THE
Real Dream

THE
Real Dream

MOLLY CONE

Illustrated by Bea Holmes

1964

HOUGHTON MIFFLIN COMPANY BOSTON
The Riverside Press Cambridge

I

THE BELL was still buzzing when Lu Martin bounded through the door, and flung herself into her seat. Hastily, she opened her book and gulped the first paragraph of the assignment. Because she should have read it yesterday, she had come early to read it today. It would have been nothing at all to finish before class — under ordinary circumstances, that is.

Lu raised her head and looked with wonder out the window. It wasn't anything you could tell anyone about. Not even Charlotte, who had lived next door to Lu all her life and was her best friend. But she guessed even Charlotte would be a bit incredulous at something like this really happening. Charlotte would say she was making it up.

Lu had to smile. The trouble was she had made it up to begin with. Or rather *him*. She had dreamed him up. She had always had a picture of him in her mind. And though she didn't expect anyone would really believe it — the dream was real. It was the boy she had seen not ten minutes ago filling out an activity ticket in front of the office in the school hall.

"Luise Martin!" called Miss Egbert, not even raising her head. She just went on making marks on the pile of papers on her desk.

Quickly Lu pulled her glance from the window. "I'm here!" she said.

Miss Egbert picked up the bunch of papers and shuffled them expertly into a neat bundle.

"I'm aware of that." Her tone was dry. "But your mind is not."

Guiltily Lu resumed her reading. But after each paragraph she covertly looked up and watched the door.

She wondered whether Miss Egbert knew that he would be coming into this room. That's what had made Lu late. He had asked Lu where Miss Egbert's room was. She had only gaped at him a moment or two before she had been able to answer sensibly.

She looked up at the door again. The hands of the electric clock jumped forward. Miss Egbert finished her work at her desk. The door remained closed. Fascinated, Lu kept her eyes on it.

She would know that she was not mistaken, she told herself, if one corner of his mouth twisted up when he smiled. That's how she would know him. Every time she had seen him in her mind's eye, his face had worn that smile.

The door swung open. The boy who stepped in scraped his feet across the threshold. The sound caused Miss Egbert to look up in surprise.

Frowning, the teacher motioned to him to come

2

forward, and he did so, placing in her outstretched hand the large white card he carried. Slowly Miss Egbert examined it. Unhurried, the boy stared back at the class.

On his head was a tattered green Tyrolean hat. A feather stuck straight up from its band. It was the sort of hat that hung in clusters next to the kewpie dolls on the novelty stands at the county fair. Miss Egbert looked up.

"Your hat," she said. "Young man, will you please remove your hat while you are in this classroom."

He looked up as if he had forgotten the hat was on his head.

His eyebrows lifted and his forehead creased trying to see the hat up there himself. He raised both hands and lifted it off. He rolled it, taking plenty of time, and stuck it into his back pocket.

Lu looked at him. Tall, but not very. Slender, but not thin. Something clicked in her mind. Dark hair, wavy; straight eyebrows and deep eyes. Another click. As Lu gazed, his mouth twisted into a lopsided grin. It sounded to Lu as though the skies were falling, but it was only the din inside her.

Miss Egbert looked up and down the rows until her glance found the empty chair next to Lu. "You may take the chair in the third row," she said to the boy.

Lu swept her purse and her extra books off the chair beside her. She wondered if everyone could hear her heart beating so loudly.

The teacher consulted the paper in her hand. "Your name is Robert Hogan," she stated as he slid into his seat.

"Yes ma'am," he said promptly.

Miss Egbert frowned. "You have never attended a Seattle school before?"

"No ma'am."

Miss Egbert looked up. "It is not necessary for you to say 'ma'am' every time you address me. Nobody around here calls me 'ma'am.'"

The new boy opened his eyes wide as he looked back at her. "Nobody calls you 'ma'am'?"

Miss Egbert shook her head, frowning at the same time at the members of the class.

Obediently, Robert Hogan nodded. "Yes sir!" he said.

Miss Egbert looked as if she had swallowed a fish-bone. She rapped on her desk with her knuckles for order.

He has a sense of humor, Lu thought, hiding her grin from Miss Egbert behind her book. She knew he would have a sense of humor.

"If you don't mind showing Robert the place in the book," she said sharply, fixing her eye on Lu, "we will continue with our reading."

Obligingly, he leaned toward her, putting his arm across the back of her chair. He nodded, as she said, a little breathlessly, "It's page sixty-five. We're supposed to finish the chapter."

He waited for her after class, as if it were the most natural thing in the world, as if he had been in the class since the day school began — as if he had waited for her always.

Walking down the hall beside her, he reached behind to the hat in his back pocket and put it on again. "Hogie is my name," he said.

"Luise," she said.

"I'm pleased to meet you, Luise," he said.

"I'm pleased to meet you too," Lu said. But she didn't tell him what she knew to be true. She had known him forever.

She walked with him to the end of the hallway, where she showed him which stairs to take.

"You're a pretty girl," he said, looking at her closely. "But what I like about you is your whispery voice. I like a girl with a whispery voice."

Lu smiled. Then ran all the way back down the hall to her next classroom.

2

As Lu BANGED into the kitchen, Mrs. Martin frowned.

"I talked with Miss Egbert today," her mother said, putting down the kettle in her hands.

Lu grimaced.

Her mother's face grew stern. "She said you dream. You look out the window — and you dream."

They expected her to be like Angie, Lu thought. Angie's only acquaintance with a 'D' was when he said *Damn*. Lu laughed at her thought.

"It's nothing to laugh about!" her mother said.

"I wasn't laughing about *that*. I was laughing about what I was thinking about."

Her mother looked at her with a puzzled expression. Miss Egbert must have told her that Lu never paid attention. It was Miss Egbert's favorite expression. *Pay attention!* As if attention was a medium of exchange. This time Lu controlled her desire to smile, and put her mind back on her mother's words.

"I don't dream," she said. And added hastily, "I guess maybe I'm just thinking about something else."

Her mother, Lu knew, was the kind who believed

6

in personal privacy. A person's room was his own, and so were his thoughts. "I found the material I wanted for my bedspread," Lu said, because she was reminded of it. "We get extra credit if we do a home project in Clothing 1."

Mrs. Martin regarded her with a new firmness. "What do you think about when you are supposed to be paying attention to Miss Egbert?" she asked.

"Things," Lu said carefully.

"What things?"

Lu hesitated. It wasn't easy to talk to your mother when she still looked at you as if your face needed washing, and she wasn't at all sure that you were capable of doing it properly yourself.

"I don't know," she said.

Her mother sat looking at her, with an odd expression of helplessness.

"I'm going to finish painting my room before I get the bedspread material," said Lu. All at once she felt a little sorry for her mother because her mother couldn't see that Lu had grown up. But another glance at her mother's face made Lu hastily take back her sympathy. Putting the thought of her mother's disapproval in the back of her mind, she went upstairs to her room.

It was such an old-fashioned room, she thought, regarding with distaste the furniture, heavy and dark, the bunches of roses on the wallpaper, and the ruffles on the window curtains. She made a face at the blue faded bedspread and the no-color paper lampshades before she dipped into one of the cans of paint she had purchased the Saturday before.

An hour later, Lu finished rolling the lovely gold color on one wall, and stepped back. The gold seemed to shimmer in the sunlight, embracing the old bureau, the desk, and the bedstand within its radiance. She would paint the old furniture white, she decided, and everything in the room would be white and gold.

She looked at the somber bureau and saw it as it would be when it was white — soft rubbed white, perhaps even with streaks of gold in it. She looked at the desk. White, too. As she gazed, the desk chair shed its brown scaly varnish and stood glistening white in the golden room. Slowly Lu turned about, seeing it all the way she wanted it to be.

There was a tap on the door. It opened and her mother stepped in — and stepped back out again.

"Oh!" Mrs. Martin said.

"I'm going to paint the furniture white," Lu said.

Mrs. Martin looked about uncertainly. "White?" She blinked at the wall.

"It's called Inca Gold," said Lu, looking at the can.

Her mother hesitated. "Don't you think the color is a little — " She raised her hand and waved it wordlessly.

Lu reminded herself that her mother was even more old-fashioned than Charlotte's mother. Charlotte used the word "square" rather than old-fashioned to describe her mother's attitude, but Lu didn't feel she should go as strongly as that even in her thoughts. She only smiled understandingly at her mother in response. And then wondered why *that* should make her mother mad.

She sighed as Mrs. Martin reminded her sharply, "Well, be sure to remember to wash out the roller after you're through here."

Lu closed the door as her mother started down the

stairs. Quickly she opened it again to shout after her, "If anyone calls, I'm right here in my room!"

Her mother paused on the stairway, looking at her strangely a moment, and without answering went on down. The extension telephone lay on a stand just across from Lu's room, right outside Angie's door. Lu looked at it reflectively a moment. With her door closed and all, she just might not hear its ring — should it ring.

She went back into her room. But she left the door open a crack, just in case.

Lu swung the roller up and down the wall thinking of Hogie. She saw his face before her, noticing the way his ears stuck close to his head. She had never thought much about a boy's ears before. Looking at the wall, she didn't really see it. She stood there smiling a long time.

At the dinner table that evening, Lu cleared her throat a couple of times. She said in a gently whispery tone, "Pass the potatoes, please."

She listened to the sound of her voice and was pleased with it. She had never thought of her voice as being whispery before. *He* had thought it was the most distinctive thing about her.

It was strange how indicative a voice was, she thought. And she considered the sound of her father's voice. He spoke crisply, the way he thought. Her mother's voice, on the other hand, was softer — not whispery, of course. But a little hesitant, as if there were lots of dots and dashes in between her phrases. She spent a lot of time on those hurried pauses.

Lu thought of Charlotte and smiled. Charlotte's voice couldn't be described as whispery at all. She talked fast and loud, and when she was excited, she shrieked.

Mrs. Martin picked up a dish and passed it to Lu. Lu looked at the dish in her hands.

With a gentleness to match the whispery note of her voice she said softly, "I said potatoes, not tomatoes."

Her mother looked at Lu. "Did you say something to me, Lu?"

Angie said, with his mouth full, "She wants someone to pass her the tomatoes."

Angie was eleven years old. His ears stuck out and his knees were knobby. He kept birds' nests in his room, was a whiz in math, and was saving for a telescope with which to examine the craters on the moon. It was difficult for Lu not to regard him with impatience.

"I did not!" said Lu. "I distinctly did not!" and then was ashamed of herself for letting her voice get out of hand. It wasn't like her, she thought. It wasn't like her at all.

Her mother went on talking to her father. Angie went on eating. The telephone rang.

"I'll get it," said Lu, pushing back her chair. She went quickly to the telephone in the kitchen.

"Hello," she said, in her whispery voice.

For an instant there was no sound at the other end of the wire. Then Charlotte's company voice came to her. "Sorry," Charlotte said, "I guess I have the wrong number."

"Charlotte?" Lu said quickly.

"Lu?" It was questioning, puzzled.

"Yes," she said throatily. "Of course it's Lu."

"You got a cold, Lu?"

An instant of impatience made her grip the telephone. "No," she said.

"Well, maybe you're just coming down with one," Charlotte diagnosed. "I thought I was getting one myself, yesterday," she offered, "but it was only my allergy."

Lu had never noticed before how curiously clear Charlotte's voice was. Almost childlike.

"I couldn't call you earlier," Charlotte said, "because I had this report to make up and — " she broke in on herself — "Who is he?"

"You mean Hogie?" Lu said, liking the sound of his name.

Charlotte sighed. "He's a *real dream*," she said.

Lu smiled into the telephone. "I know he is."

Mrs. Martin called from the other room, "Lu! Your dinner."

Lu said in a hurry, "We're still eating dinner. I'll call you later."

She came back into the dining room and sat down.

12

So far, she thought, regarding her plate, she had eaten nothing but tomatoes. She helped herself to the platter of pot roast.

"Delicious," Lu said, enjoying the sound of her voice.

"Are you getting a cold, Lu?" her father asked. She frowned at her plate. "No," she said.

"Maybe she's studying too hard," said Angie, and grinned at her from around the rim of his milk glass.

She pretended not to hear. She cast around for something to take their attention off her. "A new boy came into Miss Egbert's class today." She smiled inside herself.

"What?" said her father.

"I think she wants you to pass her some more tomatoes," said Angie with a sly grin.

Lu pressed her lips together. She moved her chair back from the table. "Will you please excuse me?" she said quite loudly, and went quickly out of the dining room up the stairs to her room.

"Hogie," she whispered into her pillow. And the name spoken in her whispery voice sent delightful prickles all the way up to the back of her neck.

3

THE CAR slowed down, made a U turn, the right tire bumping over the curb and onto the grass strip before the car raced back up the street.

Lu stopped to watch. The car screeched to a stop beside her.

"Hi!" said Hogie, sticking his head out the window to call to her.

She smiled back.

"I waited around school, looking for you," he said.

"I hurried out to buy something." She shifted the books and package in her arms. "I didn't know you were waiting."

He reached over and flipped open the door. "Well you know it now. Come on, I'll drive you home."

She walked around the car and slid into the front seat beside him. "This is a one-way street," she reminded him. "You're facing the wrong way." She pointed to the large black arrow on the street sign.

Slamming the door shut, he made another U turn, and stopped the car facing the other way. "Happy?"

Lu grinned. "They're very strict about things like that here."

He shook his head. "Crazy town," he said. His woeful expression made her laugh.

He turned the corner as she directed and went up the hill.

"I live in the two-story white house right over there," she said pointing. But he stopped before they reached it.

There were low hills in the distance, and a mist. It often rained in Seattle in January. But it wasn't raining that day. That day, thought Lu, was the most beautiful January day she had ever seen.

"You can see Mount Rainier from here, when it's out," she said, pointing to the south. "It looks like a strawberry ice-cream cone sometimes when the sun goes down."

"Out?" He looked vainly in the direction she had pointed.

She laughed. "When you've lived all your life in Seattle that's the way you talk. We celebrate when the mountain comes *out* — out of the mist that is."

A large green bus rolled to a stop behind them, its motor snorting. The driver pressed on the horn.

"We're parked in a bus zone!" cried Lu.

Hogie jerked the car forward. The driver frowned at them as he rolled by, and for no reason they laughed loudly together.

15

"Thanks for the ride," Lu said as he stopped in front of her house.

He touched her shoulder with one finger. "You going to the library tonight?"

"I might," she said.

He smiled his lopsided smile. "Maybe I'll see you there," he said.

She stood there on the curb, and watched him as he roared up the street in his little car. Then, hugging her package and books to her, she went up the walk to her house. Softly she closed the door behind her.

"Lu?" her mother's voice came from the kitchen.

"I'm home!" shouted Lu, and glanced at herself in the mirror.

She was still smiling a soft little smile, and she said as her mother came into the hallway, "I got it!" Pretending the smile was about something else.

Her mother looked a little surprised. "Got what?"

Lu plopped her books and her package down on the chair, slid out of her coat, and pulled the package from underneath the books. "The material for my bedspread. It's perfect!" Her voice had a little lilt to it that had nothing to do with the bedspread. "It's absolutely perfect." Her fingers were excited too, she reflected, for they shook a little as she tore off the wrapping.

"White!" her mother exclaimed. "You're going to make your bedspread *white!*"

16

"Gold walls," said Lu. "White bedspread — gold and white."

"Yes, I know," said her mother, but she sounded doubtful. She picked up a corner of the material and rubbed the fabric between her fingers.

"Polished cotton," said Lu, enjoying the silky shine as her mother turned it over. "All I have to do is cut it into two widths and make a seam down the center." Lu saw it suddenly as it would be on her bed, a white silken throw, softly lustrous against the golden walls.

But her mother's face did not mirror her own happy vision. It looked only stiffly blank. "Don't get pins all over the floor," she said in a tone that matched her face.

Lu wrapped the paper around it again. "I'll just cut it and pin it now," she said over her shoulder.

"How about your lessons?" her mother called after her.

Lu leaned over the bannister and shouted down. "I'll do them at the library, tonight!"

But it wasn't the bedspread she was thinking of as she stretched the material out on the bed — it was Hogie, and meeting him at the library.

She basted with long loose stitches, hurriedly. The basting wasn't too important anyway. It was only to hold the two sides together until she could stitch the seam on the sewing machine. It was an opinion her mother wouldn't agree with, thought Lu. But then, she really didn't expect her mother to approve of it anyway. Their tastes were different.

She wondered what Charlotte would say when she saw the effect the silky throw would make against the gold wall. Lu moved her needle more rapidly and ended up with a stitch almost three inches long. It would do, she thought, as she reinforced the ends with a few straight pins. She threw it over the bed. The seam in the middle where she had basted was hardly noticeable when she smoothed it down carefully. A pin slipped out, and picking it up, she stood a moment considering the blue braided rug on the floor next to her bed. She rolled it up, and stuck it into her closet. There was a white nylon rug in the bathroom. She brought it into her room and set it down beside the bed.

She stood in the middle of the room and looked about her. Her gaze settled on the lampshades. On an impulse, she smoothed out the heavy brown paper in which the fabric had been wrapped and laid it on the floor. She stirred the gold paint, and rolled it over the paper. While it was drying, she scraped a little of the worn dark varnish off the corner of the chair and daubed it, experimentally, with a bit of white enamel she had found in the basement.

Then she went back to the lampshades. The paper was almost dry, and by handling it carefully, she was able to cut it, and wrap a piece around each lampshade. The effect was pretty good, she thought.

Hearing her father's step on the stairs, she flung open her door wide. "Come see my room!"

"You don't mean you've already finished painting your room!" His face was surprised as he came to the top of the stairs.

"Almost," she said, stepping aside for her father to enter.

He stopped in the middle of the doorway and looked quickly around.

"Surprised?" she said.

He cleared his throat. "Well, yes, you might say that," he said.

Lu looked around with the finished picture of the room firmly fixed in her mind. "White and gold! That is, as soon as I finish painting the furniture white."

He regarded the several cans of paint on the floor.

"I bought it myself," she reminded him. "All of it, out of my own money. I'm doing it all myself, too."

But evidently he was not thinking about the paint. "Miss Egbert," he said.

Lu made a little church of her fingers and examined the spire. Her mother must have told him everything Miss Egbert had said.

"Do you need help with your work at school?" he asked kindly.

Lu shook her head.

"Perhaps if you tried a little harder — " he suggested, his voice gentle.

19

Lu gazed down at her gold-daubed fingertips, feeling that she should feel guilty, but somehow unable to. It was as if her feelings were unpredictable even to herself. It was almost as if they were not wholly her own and had to be sorted out like so many eggs, brown from white, large from small, before they could be labeled and held out for people to see. She smiled at the thought and her father looked surprised.

Feeling guilty about that, then, she said quickly, "I'll try!"

He nodded, pleased, she could see. He looked around the room clearing his throat again. "Well, it's certainly going to look fine in here — someday."

He closed the door behind him. Lu picked up the roller and made a few more swipes on the wall. There was a loud rap on the door, and the roller in her hand edged sloppily onto the woodwork. "Come in!" she shouted as she tried to wipe off the smudge with a rag.

"Hi," said Angie, standing in the doorway. "Would you like to order your Christmas cards?" he asked.

Lu felt her shoulders twitch. "Christmas cards! It's January."

"I get a percentage," he said, coming in and showing her an illustrated folder. "Beautiful colored cards with inspiring messages. Sell them to your friends. Order by the fifties or hundreds. A cinch to sell." Eagerly he added in his normal tone — "All I have to do is sell three dozen boxes and I'll practically have enough to buy my telescope."

20

She frowned at him. "Does Mother know you're out bothering people with Christmas cards in January?"

"I'll tell you what — " he said, ignoring the question. "I'll let you be my first customer."

"Even if I wanted to, I couldn't," she said. "I've got my whole allowance for the next two months tied up in paint and bedspread material." She rolled the roller up and down the wall again over a spot she saw she had missed the day before.

"Wow!" he said.

"It does make a bit of a difference, doesn't it?" She turned to smile at him.

But his attention was on the folder in his hands. He went out and left the door open behind him. She followed him to the doorway. "Ask Mother, before you order those things," she warned.

Angie crossed the hallway to his own room, and closed his door on her words. Lu's eyes fell on the telephone stand next to Angie's door. She crossed quickly and dialed.

"Charlotte?" She nodded at the response. "Come on over a minute." Then Lu ran downstairs to let Charlotte in.

"What do you think?" asked Lu, throwing open the door of her room. She looked at the desk, seeing it already white, at the half-made bedspread already finished in her mind's eye. She would have to do something about the window curtains, of course, and she pretended they were not there, blotted out by the golden radiance of the room. Happily she contemplated the paper-covered lampshades.

Charlotte looked about — and hesitated.

"Don't look at the details," Lu urged. "Just sort of half-close your eyes so you can get the total effect."

Charlotte turned slowly around, squinting into the corners of the room. Then she opened her eyes wide and sighed. "I don't know," she said. "I can only see it exactly the way it is. I've never been able to visualize anything." She plopped down on the middle of the new bedspread.

"I've always known exactly what I want," Lu said, but suddenly it was not the room she was thinking of.

"I have to *see* what I want, before I go after it," Charlotte said.

Lu looked at her closely. Charlotte was talking about something else too.

"What's up?" Lu asked.

Charlotte's grin suddenly covered her whole face. "I've signed up for the Junior Achievers!"

Junior Achievement was an after-school group. The boys and girls got together to form companies, and make things to sell to learn principles of business. It attracted a good many boys.

"Oh! I see!" said Lu, and then pretended she didn't. "I mean — learning about stocks and bonds and manufacturing and things. It sounds interesting."

"It sounds very interesting to me," Charlotte said.

23

"I'm in a group of ten. Eight boys!" She jumped off the bed. "I guess I'm really the business type," she said, looking at herself in the mirror. She smiled when she said, "Tonight's my Junior Achievement night. We meet every Thursday."

Lu said, "I'm going over to the library to study to-night."

Charlotte looked at her eagerly. "Do you think you might see Hogie?"

Lu patted the basted seam where it gapped on the bedspread. "I might," she said, with a little smile.

Angie hollered at them from somewhere down-stairs — "Charlotte's supposed to go home!"

Lu walked down the stairs with Charlotte, through the kitchen, to the back door.

"Dinner's almost ready," Mrs. Martin said.

Lu nodded. As she was setting the table, she won-dered suddenly what her mother would say if she knew that Lu was really in love.

4

H_E was there on the library steps waiting for her. and she hurried a little, waving to him.

He lifted his eyebrows in answer to her greeting and came running down the steps to meet her.

"Hi," he said, smiling the lopsided smile, and Lu smiled back, narrowing her eyes a little as she looked at him, thinking she would have known him anywhere.

A crowd of students swirled past them, and Lu and Hogie followed them into the library. There was a preoccupied quiet about the place, an atmosphere that was as much a part of libraries, thought Lu, as the books on the shelves.

"Where shall we sit?" Hogie nudged her.

The librarian tapped him on the shoulder. "Please keep your voice down," she cautioned, and indicated the tables around which boys and girls sat studying.

Hogie frowned back at her.

Lu led him to two empty chairs at the end of one of the long tables. "We're not supposed to talk here," she whispered behind her hand. "It's for study only."

Hogie nodded. They sat down and opened their books. Hogie hunched his chair forward. It made a loud scraping noise on the floor.

Lu looked at her book again.

Hogie opened his notebook. "I can't study when it's so quiet!" he wrote across the paper and placed it before her.

Lu smiled sympathetically as the boy next to her pulled the note toward him. He read it, added something to it, and passed it on. He grinned at Hogie. The third boy read it and passed it down once more. The paper made its way, in this manner, around the table and across to the next one. Some students added a word or two. Others merely read and sent it along. Lu went back to her book.

A little later Lu looked up and around, feeling a muffled restlessness in the room. She heard an unusual shifting of chairs.

The librarian glanced up from her desk and looked around the room. Several students were bringing armloads of books to the tables. Hogie was sprawled over his notebook, his elbow and arm resting on the table. His books were piled up precariously near the edge of the table, thought Lu, and she pushed them in toward the center. But when she looked again a moment later, they were close to the edge again.

Hogie looked up from his studying. "Is something the matter?" he asked in his normal tone of voice. As he spoke his elbow hit the books and the books hit the floor. As if it were a signal, books slammed to the floor in all parts of the big room.

The librarian rushed out from behind the desk. "Who did that!" she said loudly, forgetting her own rules.

The boys at Lu's table laughed out loud. The librarian came flying across the room toward them.

Hogie bent down to pick up his books from the floor. "It was an accident," he said.

But the librarian laid her hand on his shoulder and pinched the cloth of his jacket.

"Out!" she said, with a jerk of her head. "Immediately!"

Lu looked at her aghast. "But he didn't do anything!" she protested.

But the librarian turned her back on both of them. Lu gathered up her books and followed Hogie out.

"Why that's terrible of her!" she said as they stood on the library steps.

Hogie straightened his jacket over his shoulders. "I've been thrown out of better libraries than this," he said amiably.

Lu smiled at him warmly. He was being a good sport about it. She had known he was a good sport. It shouldn't have surprised her.

Hogie looked back over his shoulder at the closed library door. "Y'know, I think you're right," he said. "I really think it was too quiet in there to study."

"But I didn't say that — you did!"

He scratched his head. "Did I?" and grinned at her. "Let's get a Coke," he said.

She ran with Hogie down the library steps. He was the most delightful boy she had ever met, she decided, enjoying a small smug feeling about *that*.

"Did you go to the public library to study in California?" she asked as they began to walk slowly up the street.

"In L.A. I didn't waste any time studying at all!" he said grimacing.

She laughed and he took her elbow and steered her across the street.

"What does your father do?" she asked. It would be nice, she thought, to move from one part of the country to another.

"He sells things," said Hogie. "He gets onto a good thing and buys the whole lot and goes around selling it. He's a born salesman," said Hogie.

"My father is in the insurance business," said Lu. She had never thought about her father's business particularly one way or another. "I guess it's a pretty good business for him — at least he's never said anything about not liking it."

"My dad is the kind that likes to keep moving," said Hogie. "When he gets onto a good deal, we just pack up the car and off we go!"

It sounded like a happy, casual way to live, Lu thought.

There was a crowd at the Coke shop before them.

"Hi, Lu!" someone called out. And she smiled and waved a hand.

Two people moved out of one of the small booths and Hogie slid in.

"Say!" said a girl shrilly. "We've been standing here waiting for this booth."

The girl beside the speaker plucked at her elbow. "Come on," she said. "There are two empty stools at the counter."

"We'll take the two stools," Lu spoke up.

The girl hesitated. Her friend went over and sat down on one of the empty stools. "The stools are okay," she said. She went over and sat down next to her friend.

"They would never have given up that easy in Chicago," said Hogie under his breath to Lu.

"You mean you really lived in Chicago?" Lu said blinking at him.

"Only for six months," he said.

"It's different in Seattle." She tried to explain something to him. "It's first come, first served. No matter who you are."

"What'll you have, kids?" The waitress made a swipe at the table top with a towel, and took out her pad.

"Two Cokes," Hogie said.

Lu opened her notebook. She made squiggles on the lined paper as they drank their Cokes.

"I have to be home by ten."

"Whatever you say," he said.

"I've never known anyone who has been to as many different places as you have." Lu played with the ice in her glass.

He said, with a little twist on his lips, "I've never really known anyone who has lived in only one place. It must be nice — I mean living in one house all your life."

He sounded wistful, thought Lu. "I guess it's six of one and a half dozen of the other. They both have advantages."

He twirled the straw around in his glass. "I'd just as soon stay in Seattle," and then, as if he had revealed too much of himself, he said, raising his voice — "but if this is the kind of service you get around here, I don't know that I will."

The waitress looked up startled.

"Did you want something?" she asked.

"The check," he said. He reached into his back pocket and pulled out some change. He said in an aside to Lu, "Most places I've been to, they give you the check before you sit down."

Lu pulled on her coat. He couldn't fool her, she thought. That loud voice was just a cover-up for the sensitivity underneath. She took a long deep breath of the cool night air, when they came out.

Hogie turned up the collar of his jacket. "Brr-r!" he said. "Who turned on the air conditioner?"

She laughed. "It's always chilly in the evenings in

Seattle. Particularly in January," she said. "After all, it's supposed to be winter." She looked at the starless sky. "It could even snow tonight."

He was incredulous. "I thought it only rained here. That's what they told us in California. In Seattle it rains in the morning, and it rains in the evening — "

"They left out the afternoon," she said interrupting him. "It even rains then sometimes. But nothing is predictable. We've had Januarys that are practically as nice as Junes.

"What kind of weather do you usually have in June?" he asked.

She grinned. "Rain or clouds. Our best part of summer comes in August and September and — "

He interrupted her with a chuckle.

"I never thought I'd find the weather such an interesting subject to talk about," he said.

The glow spread through her. It was a compliment, the nicest compliment she had ever received.

They walked back to the library where he had parked his car. Stopping in front of her house, they sat out in the car talking until a few minutes before ten, then he walked with her to the door.

"You're nice," he said. "You're the nicest girl I've ever known." He pulled at her hand, pulling her close to him.

Lu held herself a little away.

"What's the matter?" he whispered. "You scared

31

I'll kiss you?"

His eyes laughed at her. He was teasing. And suddenly she could answer honestly.

"I think kissing should be something special," she said.

"For you it is special," he said huskily. He kissed her lightly, reverently, on her lips.

Lu opened her eyes. It was just exactly as she had expected it to be.

The front door opened wide. "Lu?" It was her mother.

"I'm just coming in, Mother," she said. "Come in and meet my mother and dad," she said to Hogie.

He followed her, blinking as they entered the light-filled room.

"Mother," she said, "Dad, this is Hogie, Robert Hogan. Hogie, this is my mother and father."

"Hello Hogie," her mother said politely. Her father said, "How do you do," and thrust out his arm for a handshake.

Hogie responded to Mr. Martin's firm clasp, staring at him with interest.

He's not afraid of people, thought Lu, and she said, trying to hide her pride in him with a little rush of words — "Hogie comes from Los Angeles. He's in Miss Egbert's class too."

Mrs. Martin smiled at him. "Well, perhaps I'll meet your mother at the P.T.A. meeting Thursday."

"No you won't," Hogie corrected her. "She stayed in California. She had a good job and she wasn't leaving it."

"Oh," said Mrs. Martin, as if she didn't quite know what to say. "That must be a little hard on you."

Hogie shrugged, elaborately, in such a comic manner, that Lu had to smile. "I'm not complaining," he said, raising his eyebrows, "especially since she's making the payments on my car."

Hogie chuckled. "It made my dad pretty mad. He figured she should have given it to him if she felt like giving cars away."

Mr. Martin gave a short laugh. "How do you and your father like living in Seattle?"

Hogie shrugged. "We've lived in a lot of different towns. There's always something the matter with every one of them, my dad thinks."

Mrs. Martin said, "We're very proud of the beauties of our city."

"You're right about that!" Hogie said, looking at Lu.

Quickly Lu said, "My little brother is asleep or he'd be down here saying hello, too."

An alert voice came from the top of the stairs. "I am not," said Angie. He came down, two steps at a time, attired in his striped pajamas. "Hi!" he said.

"Hi," said Hogie, and grinned at him. "You don't look much like your sister."

"I'm the one with the brains," Angie said modestly.

Lu made a face at her brother. Mr. Martin put a hand on Angie's shoulder. "Up to bed with you," he said, his voice surprisingly sharp.

Hogie and Lu had a glass of milk and a cookie in the kitchen, and Lu walked with him to the door. She walked across the porch with him.

"Goodnight," she said softly, and with the shadow of the smile on her face, came back into the house and closed the door behind her.

Her father yawned elaborately. "Whatever happened to that nice redheaded boy who used to hang around here?" he asked.

Lu looked at her parents. She couldn't even remember who they were talking about. They both gazed back at her brightly, as if they expected her to answer the question.

She turned and ran up the stairway. In her room, she stared out into the darkness of the night a moment before switching on the light.

The telephone rang. Lu went out into the hall to answer it.

"Lu?" Charlotte's eager voice held a question in it.

"It's me," said Lu, dully.

"Did Hogie bring you home?"

"Yes," said Lu.

"What did your parents think?"

"They didn't like him," said Lu. "They didn't like him at all," and putting the telephone back on the table, she went into her room and closed the door.

5

"They're just acting like parents," Charlotte consoled her when they talked about it as they did every day throughout the whole next week. "My mother would flip if she thought I was crazy about some boy."

Lu corrected her. "I didn't say I was crazy about him. All I did was introduce him."

"To parents, it's practically one and the same thing," Charlotte said wisely. "Probably they can't stand the thought of your growing up."

Lu shook her head. "They *want* me to grow up. That's what they talk about all the time — growing up to my responsibilities — like paying attention to Miss Egbert."

"It's not the same thing at all," said Charlotte. "They want you to *act* like you're grown up, but they don't much care to have you *feel* you're grown up."

"I don't feel grown up at all," Lu said, trying to analyze her feelings. "I feel just sort of — desperate."

Charlotte bounced up and down on the bed. "That's it!" she said. "That's it, exactly. That's the way all grownups feel!" She looked at Lu enviously.

"And to think you didn't even have to join the Junior Achievers or anything like that."

Lu looked up quickly, "Why don't I?" she said, feeling suddenly as if she had the answer to something that needed a solution.

"Why don't you what?" Charlotte looked at her with her mouth still open.

"Join the Junior Achievers," said Lu, sitting up straighter. "Me and Hogie too, that is. Hogie talks a lot about business," she added conscientiously.

Charlotte looked at her reflectively. "You mean then you could see him a lot, and your parents couldn't very well say anything about your not seeing him so often."

Lu clasped her knees to her chin. There was an uncomfortable feeling at the pit of her stomach. "It isn't that I want to deceive them," she said, and knew that this was true. "But — " she blinked as she felt her nose grow stuffy and had trouble keeping the tears out of her eyes — "I've got to keep seeing him; I've just got to!" And strangely she knew this too was every bit as true.

Charlotte said in awe, "You mean they forbade you to see him?"

Lu laughed hoarsely. "They're too smart for that!" In a way she wished they had, for that would have been something definite, and something, therefore, she could fight against.

Charlotte leaned toward her. "What did they say?"

"It isn't what they *say!*" said Lu. "It's what they *don't* say. It comes through," she said darkly. "It comes through loud and clear. You should see their faces every time the phone rings." She added bitterly, "It isn't even *him* half the time."

"Who is it?" Charlotte asked breathlessly.

"You," Lu said.

Charlotte looked disappointed.

Lu leaned over Charlotte. Pulling a tissue from the box on the nightstand, she blew her nose. The telephone rang, and Lu knocked the box off the bureau as she dashed to answer it. But her mother had picked up the kitchen telephone already.

". . . terribly early for Christmas cards," Lu caught the second half of a sentence, and she set the receiver down again.

"I never heard of anyone joining the Junior Achievement group once it is started," Charlotte said doubtfully as Lu returned to the room.

"Well, you did," Lu looked at her friend suspiciously.

"We meet tomorrow night," Charlotte said quickly. "And I'll ask. We meet every Thursday evening," she explained, "for business meetings, and as soon as we decide what we want to manufacture, we'll have to meet almost every night after school for a while to get into production."

"I don't mind working after school every night!"

Lu said quickly, thinking about seeing Hogie that often.

Conspiratorially Charlotte squeezed her hand. "I'll talk to the adviser," she said, and grinned at Lu.

Lu walked downstairs with Charlotte and said good-bye to her at the front door. Sighing, she went into the kitchen.

Her mother sat before the telephone. "Do you know anything about some Christmas cards Angie has been selling around the neighborhood?" she asked Lu.

Lu opened the refrigerator door, shrugging in response to her mother's question. She found an apple, and bit into it.

"He tried to sell me not long ago," she said.

"I don't believe in taking advantage of one's friends and neighbors by trying to sell them something," Mrs. Martin said.

Lu looked at her mother's serious face. "They're only Christmas cards," she pointed out. "Everybody buys Christmas cards. For that matter," she added, "everybody sells them, too."

"Well, that's all right for those really in need," said Mrs. Martin.

"I guess that's the way Angie figures it," said Lu. "He thinks he needs a telescope more than anything."

Her mother's mouth grew firm. "He'll just have to earn it some other way," she said. "I don't approve of children selling door-to-door."

Lu had stopped listening. She stood gazing out of the window. She heard her mother sigh as she turned away.

"I don't suppose you'd mind," Lu began, her voice a little shaky, "if I join Charlotte's Junior Achievement group, would you?" And for no special reason, Lu felt her heart begin to thump uncertainly.

Her mother turned about, relief flooding her face. "Why, I think that would be a splendid idea!" she said wholeheartedly.

Lu nodded, and not meeting her mother's eyes, walked quickly out the back door and over to Charlotte's.

6

Impatiently, Lu endured the morning at school until she could see Hogie. At the noon hour, after lunch, they strolled across the grounds behind the school.

"We're really not supposed to leave the building at noon," Lu told him conscientiously, but she did not turn back. "Everything smells green," she said, sniffing deeply.

Hogie poked at her. "Next thing you'll say is that everything tastes pink!"

Lu looked at him surprised, and chuckled. It was a nice idea, and she liked it.

"You're right," she said happily. "It's a pink day." She smiled at him.

It was a cold clear day with gusty breezes. The mountain had come out from behind the clouds; Lake Washington rippled blue in the sharp sunshine.

"We get our very best views of the mountains on winter days," said Lu, and Hogie grinned at her as if she had said something funny.

He really didn't care whether the skies were gray or blue, she thought fondly, or whether or not the mountain could be seen. She told him about Charlotte's Junior Achievement group.

"They're just starting," she said, "and if we could get in, it might be fun."

"Sounds okay to me," he said, not really caring.

"You'll learn all about business," she said, making a face at him. "It's very important to know all about business."

He looked at her with his crooked smile. "Now you sound just like my father," he said. "He's plenty smart about business."

Lu told him how her mother had forbidden Angie to sell Christmas cards because she thought it wasn't nice. She giggled a little at her own interpretation, knowing it was not exactly true.

"She interferes a lot, doesn't she?" Hogie said.

Lu stood still. "That's not interfering," she said. "After all, Angie is only eleven. She has a right to tell him what to do."

Hogie tossed his books on the grass and sat down on an outcropping of rocks. "I guess I was pretty lucky," he said. "My mother didn't care what I did."

He sounded so pleased that Lu tried not to show how shocked she felt. She put her books down, and sat down beside him.

"I care," she said. "I'd hate to have you do things that I didn't think were right."

He looked at her reflectively. "I never thought of it that way," he said. He looked away, squinting again at the sun moving in behind a cloud. "I guess my mother wasn't much like yours," he said, his face

smoothing out as the cloud hid the sun entirely. He
took his hat out of his pocket and placed it on his head.
He said casually, "I never saw much of her anyway.
I hung around my dad most of the time."

"Like Angie," said Lu, thinking how Angie heard
his father when he never seemed to hear anyone else.

Hogie grinned. "When I was little, I thought my
dad was a giant. Whenever he talked to me, he yelled."

"My father yells, too," Lu put in — "at Angie."

"It used to scare me when my father yelled — really
yelled, I mean. It used to scare me to death."

"I hate to hear my father yelling even when it's not at me," said Lu.

"Most times my father talks loud on purpose. Like to the landlord. He figures if he keeps him scared, he might forget to ask for the rent. My father is pretty smart sometimes," he said with pride.

Suddenly Lu felt sorry for Hogie. Sorry because he wanted to be proud of his father and he couldn't be. She plucked a bit of lint off his sweater sleeve.

Hogie turned his head, looking down at her fingers on his sleeve. "What gets me is why I put up with a girl like you," he said grinning a little. "You never even let me kiss you much!"

Lu laughed out loud, and jumped up. She climbed to the top of the rocks, and stood there, looking out over the green lawns of the school, over the low roofs of the gymnasium building, out to the water, rimmed with hills.

Hogie stood below her, looking up at her. Glancing at him, she saw the admiration shining in his eyes. She jumped down and picked up her books.

"You're sort of a dream girl," he said.

Lu felt a catch in her throat. "You're a bit of a dream come true, yourself," she whispered, just as the sharp buzz of the school bell warned the end of lunch period.

They hurried to reach the side entrance of the school building. He pushed at the door and went in, and she followed him, frowning a little.

44

"You're supposed to let ladies go first," she said.
"Who said so?"

"I said so," Lu said.

"Okay, princess," he said, and grinned back. He opened the inner door for her, stood back, and allowed her to precede him.

"Okay, princess?" he whispered, as they joined the throngs in the hall.

She nodded, and felt like a princess as he guided her through the crowds of students. He left her at her classroom door, and she waved goodbye.

At her desk she opened her notebook, looking at the assignment on the blackboard. But what she saw was Hogie looking at her as he did when she stood up there on the rocks. As the teacher's voice began to drone forth, she heard above it, Hogie's hoarse whisper. "Princess," he had said. He had called her "princess."

There was a peculiar silence about her. Lu blinked and looked around the room.

Everyone was looking at her. Here and there was a grin, a warning smile. But there was no smile on Mr. Hanley's face.

"Are you with us, Luise?" Mr. Hanley's words were spoken in a hushed voice as if he might be afraid of waking somebody up. The class laughed.

Lu sat straight and nodded.

"Thank you," he said politely, and Lu felt her face grow warm.

"The subject of discussion was grades," said Mr. Hanley. "Admittedly," he said and raised his eyebrows, directing his glance toward Lu, "there are some of us here who are not much interested, but to those who are, I would like to explain how we arrive at what we call a 'grade' and just why this conceivably might be important to each and every one of you."

Lu endured the rest of the period. World history was an old and dead thing, she thought. And it was with difficulty that she followed the discourse on events that had happened a hundred years before. What interested her was what was happening today and yesterday — real, earnest, wonderful things.

She shook herself and picked up the last part of Mr. Hanley's question. She wrote the words in her notebook because everyone else seemed to be doing that, and as the buzzer sounded marking the period's end, she jumped up.

"Hey!" said the boy who sat behind her. "Do you know we're in three classes together?"

She smiled vaguely. "Excuse me," she said, "but I promised to meet someone." She hurried out of the classroom, wondering whether Charlotte had found out whether her Junior Achievement group would take any new members.

Lu made her way through the crowds to the landing where Charlotte would be coming down on her way to her next class, while she would be going up.

7

"WELCOME!" said a thin man with a mustache of hair over his forehead. "Welcome to the Misco Company of the Junior Achievement!" He nodded to Lu and Hogie, sitting together at one end of the table. "My name is George Potsdam."

Hogie choked suddenly, clutching his shirt over his chest in a fit of coughing. Lu looked at him sympathetically, and Charlotte handed him her clean handkerchief.

Mr. Potsdam waited kindly. "Are you all right, young man?"

Hogie nodded, wiping the tears from his eyes. "Swallowed my gum," he explained.

All of the boys laughed except one, who looked somewhat like a senior edition of Angie. He merely looked at Hogie with interest.

"May I suggest, Mr. Potsdam, that we all introduce ourselves, before we inform our new members of the progress made up to this point," he said.

Mr. Potsdam beamed at the boy, and Charlotte sitting next to him, made a face. She doesn't like him,

47

thought Lu, and looking around, knew all at once that there wasn't one boy here that Charlotte really liked. She looked at her friend sympathetically.

"Since I proposed it, I will begin," the boy who looked like Angie said. "My name is William Allen."

"John Collins."

"Anthony Teebruck."

"Sonny Evans."

Lu hid her smile. That one didn't even come up to Charlotte's chin.

"Robert Watkins," said the boy next to Lu. Quickly she said, "Luise Martin."

"Robert Hogan!" said Hogie loudly. And Mr. Potsdam nodded, and listened attentively to the next two names. "I always like to place a name firmly in my mind," he said. "It's good policy."

"We seem to be very fortunate," he went on, "to have gained two new members for our company at the very time we unfortunately lost two. The Gaynor twins will no longer be with us."

Curiously Lu glanced at Charlotte. She looked crestfallen. She liked one of *them* the best, Lu thought, and felt sorry for her friend.

"What's Misco?" Lu asked at the next pause.

Charlotte answered her. "Short for Miscellaneous Company," Charlotte said proudly. She didn't have to tell them. Anyone could see it was her idea.

"It was a compromise," the boy called William Allen explained carefully. "We couldn't decide what to make, so we decided on a name that will fit anything we decide on."

All the companies met once a week for business meetings, she learned, usually from seven to nine in the evening. Each chose a product to manufacture — bottle racks, centerpieces, candle holders, patio lights, spice racks — things like that. What was made wasn't really as important as learning how a company gets organized to make something. They operated exactly the way a real company did. Each Junior company had a real company as a sponsor and the real company advised them. After they organized, they sold stock and got into production and out of the profits, they paid dividends.

"A cutting board . . ." said William Allen. "I move that we adopt a cutting board in the shape of a pig as our product to sell."

No one could think of anything better, although Lu reflected with a small smile that Hogie had come up with some marvelous suggestions that had added spice to the dry discussion. A pot-watcher, for instance, to keep pots from boiling over.

The motion on the cutting board was passed. William Allen was appointed manager in charge of sales. Charlotte was dubbed his assistant; mostly because those two had talked so much, Lu decided privately.

It was a very interesting meeting, Lu told her mother and father with real enthusiasm, but she didn't tell them Hogie had been there.

"It's a fine organization for high school students," her father said.

Lu watched her mother and father exchange satisfied looks. They think I've forgotten all about Hogie, she thought, and feeling uncomfortable under their approving gazes, she went up to bed.

8

CHARLOTTE sat on Lu's bed with her legs crossed and her elbows resting on her knees. "I've got to think of some sales ideas." She looked glum. "I have to think of something in the next fifteen minutes. The sales advertising meeting is at my house."

Lu combed her hair and thought of Hogie waiting for her every day after Miss Egbert's class and walking with her to the next class. It was too bad they had only one class together, she thought. When you really like someone, seeing him only once or twice a day, and only one evening a week from seven to nine just wasn't enough. In the three weeks since they had become Junior Achievers they had been so busy that they had hardly had a chance to even take much of a ride after school. There were all those maple boards that had to be cut into pig shapes, and oiled and rubbed to make ready for the Junior Achievement Trade Fair.

"The Trade Fair is in two weeks," Charlotte said darkly. "The company that's making patio lights are dressing in hula skirts and Hawaiian shirts, with a grass hut and everything — to help sell their stuff."

"Well, wearing cowboy shirts and jeans while we sell our little pigs wasn't such a bad idea," Lu pointed out. That was Hogie's idea, she thought proudly. And his mother had sent him a real dude ranch outfit with boots and everything. "We can go really down at the farm — and all that."

Charlotte turned an accusing eye on her. "We could," she sniffed, "if your boyfriend weren't getting so dandied up that the rest of us will look like poor-relation cowhands." Charlotte wrinkled her forehead. "What we need is something real! Something that'll make people sit up and take notice."

It occurred to Lu that she could see Hogie at the basketball game the next night. It was the first game played at the home school. Her activity ticket covered all the games too. She smiled.

"You've got one?" Charlotte said eagerly.

"Got what?"

"An idea. I've got to come up with something fast."

Lu conscientiously put her thoughts on the matter of the cutting board shaped like a pig. "Why don't we get hold of a real live pig to display?" she said suddenly.

"What for?"

"To attract attention to our booth where we'll be dressed like cowhands selling cutting-board pigs."

Charlotte considered it. "Well, at least it's an idea," she said grudgingly.

Lu regarded her with a bit of impatience. "I

thought that was what your meeting today was for —
to talk over ideas."

"That's what it's for all right." Charlotte shuddered. "Imagine having to spend a whole afternoon with William Allen!"

Lu patted her shoulder, and decided to be kinder to her friend.

"Out of eight boys in the company, it's just my luck to draw William Allen," said Charlotte. "That's all he talks about, business!"

Lu grinned. "Well, that's what he's coming over for, isn't it?"

Charlotte pulled herself up off the bed. "You bet it is," she said, and clomped down the stairs to keep her appointment.

Thinking her own thoughts, Lu followed her down.

"How are you getting along with Miss Egbert?" her mother asked when Lu wandered into the kitchen.

Lu flushed. Not because she hadn't been paying attention to Miss Egbert, but because Miss Egbert's name reminded her of Hogie — and even the very thought of Hogie seemed to affect her strangely.

"Fine," she said, and for no reason that Lu could see, her mother sighed.

The telephone rang, and Lu jumped. Her mother picked it up and handed it to her with an odd expression on her face.

"Hello?" Lu said, barely breathing.

It was only Charlotte. "The committee passed on and adopted your pig idea!" she said. "I said it was your idea," she said loyally. "And you've been unanimously elected to help on the sales advertising committee."

Quickly she looked over her shoulder to where her mother stood at the sink. "How about . . ." she began.

"Just a minute."

Lu held the telephone, hearing only sibilant sounds over the wire.

"Hogie, too," Charlotte's voice came on again. "But he's got to be serious," she warned in exact imitation of William Allen's solemn tones. Lu smiled happily.

"And now the question is — where can we get a pig?" Charlotte waited.

Mrs. Martin's curious gaze prompted Lu to say, "It's Charlotte. She wants to know where we can get a live pig. It's for our display at the Junior Achievement Trade Fair."

"Let me see now," said Mrs. Martin, looking around the kitchen as if she were trying to remember where she might have put a pig. "There's a farm out north of Bothell that raises litters of pigs. I remember now. We saw them there when we drove out into the country for fresh eggs a couple of Sundays ago."

Lu spoke into the telephone. "There's a farm out past Bothell — " she began.

Charlotte interrupted her. "Look Lu, why don't you come with us and show us where. Wait a minute — "

Charlotte's voice came again. "That will be just fine, William says," said Charlotte loudly. Her voice dropped to a whisper. "Lu, come with us — please?"

Lu hesitated. Charlotte said, "William will call Hogie and we'll pick him up too."

"All right," Lu said, and feeling only a little troubled, she told her mother where they were going. It wasn't as if *she* had invited Hogie, she decided.

Sitting beside Hogie, in the back seat of William's car, Lu smiled into the collar of her coat.

William was sixteen and a junior. He frowned as he drove, staring straight ahead, gazing at each stoplight as if it might change color unexpectedly. Lu caught Hogie's expression and turning her head, smiled out the window.

William cleared his throat. "In case you're worried, or anything, I'm a very careful driver."

Charlotte raised her eyebrows at Lu.

"The pig idea is capital," William said, as if he were conducting a regular meeting. "It's got everything — appeal, action, appropriateness and economy. That is," he qualified, "if we can borrow it instead of buy it."

"Big Business with a Capital B," Hogie put in.

"That's right," said William, not seeing anything funny. "That's it exactly."

Lu looked out the window, not trusting herself to look at Hogie. But she was smiling anyway.

"What you want is a weaner pig," said the big woman who wore an apron over a pair of blue jeans.

Lu and Charlotte looked at each other. "You mean they make weiners out of pigs!" said Charlotte.

The woman laughed. "A weaner pig is a pig that's just been *weaned*," she said. "They're not very old."

She led them out to the pen. "I don't mind lending you one," she said, "seeing it's for a good cause."

"We'll take very good care of it," Charlotte said.

"You got a pen to keep it in?"

"It won't take me long to make one," William said. "I'm taking shop."

The woman snorted. "You don't need a regular workshop to make a pigpen. A good big crate will do if you haven't got something handier. It'll do for a while anyway. They aren't very active." She looked at Hogie. "Unless you scare them."

Hogie smiled back at her, but he hadn't been listening. He had been looking past her, up toward the house. In the middle of the front yard was a low red and black sports car, sitting like a rooster in the center of a barnyard.

The woman led them over to a pen full of small pigs. "We're sending the whole kit and kaboodle of them out tomorrow morning, so if you want one, you'd better take it while the taking's good. We don't usually keep them here to fatten them up."

Lu looked around. Hogie had not come with them. He was strolling instead up toward the house. As she watched, he reached the car, and stood gazing at it. Lu turned back to the others, smiling to herself.

Lu looked over the fence. The little animals snuffling and grunting had black hairy heads, a broad pink stripe around their middle and dirty pink feet. They didn't look the way she had expected pigs to look.

Charlotte said, with a puzzled air, "I thought pigs were round and smooth and pink."

The woman made a sound which might have been a laugh. "These are belted hogs," she said. "Which one you want?"

"That one," Charlotte said, pointing to the smallest of the lot. "Let's have that one."

"You mean the runt?" asked the woman.

"He's not a runt!" said Charlotte. "He's just darling."

The woman grinned. "The smallest one of the litter is always called the runt."

William said, "Is it all right if we take that one?"

"Take any one you want," she said waving her arms. "I'll go into the house and get something to put him in."

William climbed over the fence.

"Here little pig," he cooed, squatting down and holding out his hand. "Come here, little pig."

58

Charlotte giggled.

"I think you're supposed to call *soo-ee* or something like that," Lu said.

"Maybe you'd better just grab him and pick him up," Charlotte said in her practical manner.

William grabbed, and the little pig let out a squeal and streaked to the other side of the pen.

William picked himself up. Lu tried not to giggle.

"He's sort of slippery," William said, frowning at them.

"Pigs are supposed to be slippery," Charlotte said, "or at least that's the way they were in the old Mother Goose rhymes."

Lu said, "I think that was a greased pig, remember?"

William said, "If you girls would mind not wasting time reminiscing and get in here and help me corner this animal — maybe we could catch him." He looked around. "Where's Hogie?"

"He's on an inspection tour of his own," said Lu, pointing to the car in the yard.

William shrugged.

Charlotte looked over her shoulder. "Maybe the lady won't mind helping us," she said, nodding at the woman crossing the yard. They waited as she came toward them, a gunnysack over her arm.

"Haven't you decided yet?" she asked them.

William said, "We've decided — but so has he. Only he's decided not to get caught."

"Pshaw!" said the woman. "You're not going about it properly. Just pick him up by the hind legs and stick him into this sack."

William's large Adam's apple moved. "You mean, pick him up by his hind legs?" His voice rose to a squeak.

"How else do you expect to pick him up?" said the woman. She handed him the sack.

William scratched his nose. "Okay," he said. He tossed the sack to Charlotte. "Here, you hold it open."

Charlotte paled. "Me?"

Lu took hold of one end of the sack. "I'll help too," she said.

The woman turned back to the house. "When you get him into the trunk of your car," she called, "stop at the house and I'll give you some stuff for his dinner."

They were all a little shaken by the time the snorting shrieking pig was tied into the sack and laid into the trunk of the car. Except Hogie. Hogie whistled happily, undisturbed by the bumping and the muffled snorting in the back.

Charlotte shivered. "I feel as if we're taking part in a trunk murder," she said. "That poor little pig."

William Allen driving carefully home again seemed to give no thought to Charlotte's feelings. "I'll bring over the scraps from our dinner table every day to feed it," he said, "just like the woman said."

Charlotte gasped. "You'll bring them over where!"

"To your house, of course."

"You mean we're going to keep the pig at *my* house!" shrieked Charlotte.

William glanced at her briefly. "I live in an apartment."

Charlotte sat still for a moment. "Maybe my mother won't let me keep a pig at our house."

"I asked her," he said. "Before we left. It's okay. Just so long as we keep it penned up and feed it ourselves."

"You mean you're coming over every day to feed it?" Charlotte's voice choked a little.

"That's my job," he said. "And yours too," he added.

Charlotte looked ruefully at Lu. Then she settled back and was silent all the rest of the way home.

Lu looked out the window, watching car after car pass them by. William at the wheel, they rattled along slowly.

"Hey!" said Hogie, pulling himself forward so he

could read the speedometer. "What speed is she good for?"

William frowned. "I've never driven her over fifty miles an hour," he said shortly.

Hogie settled back. He glanced sideways at Lu, grimacing. Lu tried not to smile.

They turned into their own neighborhood.

"You want to go with me to the basketball game tomorrow night?" Hogie whispered to Lu.

She smiled. "All right."

"It's a date," he told her as they left him on the corner near the school.

9

Lu came to a decision about things before she had even realized she had. "I'm going to the basketball game with Hogie," she said bravely. "He's going to pick me up."

Her mother came down the stairs slowly. She didn't say anything right away. Her father, sitting in the living room reading his newspaper, lowered it, looking up. Her parents exchanged glances.

They don't want me to go, but they're not going to say no, thought Lu, feeling the communication between them. And she felt, suddenly, relief. They weren't going to say no, positively. She smiled warmly at first one parent, then the other.

"I suppose that boy will come for you in his car," her mother said.

Lu put her smile away. "His name's Hogie," she said. "All the kids go to the games in their cars."

Her mother said quickly, "You look very nice."

But Lu pretended not to hear. She went into the living room and sat down and picked up a magazine.

Mr. Martin lowered his newspaper. "So you're going to the basketball game."

Lu nodded.

"I used to be a pretty good basketball player myself," her father said, too heartily.

Lu sighed. "Yes Daddy, I know." She put the magazine down.

The door slammed. Angie came in. "Hey!" he said. "Do you know there's a basketball game at your school tonight?"

"Hogie is picking me up," Lu said.

The telephone rang. She hurried into the kitchen to answer it.

"Lu?" It was Charlotte. "I thought you were going to the basketball game."

"I am," Lu said. "I'm waiting for Hogie."

"I'm not going." Charlotte's voice dropped to a whisper. "William Allen is here. He is sitting out with the pig. He thinks it might be lonely."

Lu smiled. "Then you might as well go to the game."

Charlotte groaned. "My mother said it isn't nice for me to go off and leave that boy sitting with the pig by himself. She says I'd better go out and keep him company."

Lu chuckled.

"I thought maybe if you weren't going to the game, you'd come over and keep *me* company," Charlotte sounded wistful.

"I'm going to the game with Hogie," Lu said gently.

A few minutes later the doorbell rang three times, one after the other. Lu flung her coat over her shoulders. "I'm going!" she called as she opened the door to Hogie.

"Have a good time," her mother said to both of them, but her face was stiff.

"Good luck to the home team!" called Mr. Martin from his chair in the living room. His voice was too loud.

"We're almost late," she said as they ran down the porch steps.

Hogie shrugged. "If I had the car, I wouldn't have been so long."

Lu looked up and down the street. "What happened to it?"

He grimaced. "Nothing much happened to it, just to *me*. They took away my license — for a month. I couldn't convince them it wasn't my fault. They sure put lights in funny places in this town."

"But if it wasn't your fault, that's not fair!"

He grinned at her warm concern. "That's what *I* told them," he said.

They walked along faster, toward the school. The basketball game was in the school gymnasium.

"What did your father say?" Lu asked.

Hogie made a face. "He says he's never gotten a ticket in his life he had to pay."

"Well, at least he didn't yell," Lu said.

"I didn't say he didn't yell," Hogie said, squinting

as if the sun were shining directly in his eyes. But the sun had set long before.

Lu glanced at him and then away. He took her arm as they came nearer the school, elbowing through the crowd of students pushing into the gymnasium.

Inside the gym, they crowded into the line at the end of one of the bleachers. Standing with the others, Lu raised her voice in the flag salute which had already begun . . . "one nation under God, indivisible . . ."

"INVISIBLE . . ." said Hogie.

Lu smiled as she went on — "with liberty and justice for all."

Miss Egbert, sitting two benches below them, turned around and fixed her stare on Hogie. The girl behind them giggled.

The school band crashed in with "The Star-Spangled Banner," and Lu sang out, pretending not to notice that Hogie was trying to inch the whole line down so they would have more room when they sat down. He has a nice voice, she thought, listening as he sang, and she smiled, as if this too was only what she had expected.

"Play ball!" shouted Hogie, his voice rising above the ordinary noise.

Faces from the rows below turned up toward them, disapproving.

Lu said, "They haven't finished the flag ceremony

yet. Nothing is supposed to start until they carry it out."

Shuffling and scraping filled the gymnasium as the standing audience sat down.

Hogie stretched out his legs and folded his arms. "They need shaking up a bit," he said out of the side of his mouth.

Lu made a face at him too, but it wasn't much of one. They didn't understand him, she thought. Not as she did. And she joined the cheer that rose as the team ran out.

"Keep your eye on Jim Haley," the boy in front of them turned to advise. "He's the whole team, if you ask me. That's Sandra Collins, sitting in the first row. She's his girl friend."

Lu looked with interest at the pretty blond girl wearing a letter sweater over her shoulders.

"PLAY BALL, Jim Haley!" Hogie stood up to shout. And the girl named Sandra Collins turned her face up to Hogie and waved.

"They're seniors," said Lu for no reason at all, and rose with the others in a shout as the referee's whistle put the ball in action.

In the third quarter of the game, something fluttered against the back of Lu's head and dropped into her lap. It was a paper airplane, and Lu stared at it in surprise. Paper throwing was not allowed at any time during a game. Rules were posted all over the gym. Hogie picked it off her lap and sent it sailing back.

Lu ducked and covered her head with her hands as it came flying back.

"They can't do that!" said Hogie. He stood up and with careful aim shot the paper toy directly into the center of the floor. There was a gasp, and the referee's whistle blew fiercely.

Startled, Lu gaped at the halted game.

Beside her, Hogie moved quickly. "Let's get out of here," he whispered, and taking her hand, pulled her quickly off the bleacher and out the exit only a few feet from where they were sitting. They ran down the steps, around the building to the next corner.

"Whew!" he said.

Lu began to laugh. She thought of Hogie foolishly protecting her by throwing back the paper plane. It was an extravagant gesture, for he could have been barred from attending any more games.

"It wasn't much of a game, anyway," said Hogie, discrediting his gallantry. "They play like a bunch of amateurs."

"You sound just like my dad," she said. "He thinks no team plays as good a game as his team did when he was in high school." Thinking about her father reminded her of Charlotte sitting at home with William Allen and the pig. She told Hogie.

He laughed. "Good old William. He's taking all this business stuff seriously."

"My father thinks it's good for a boy to learn about business," Lu said, but she looked at him with understanding.

"Well, that's where your dad and mine are in agreement," he said. "I've got to get me a job, pronto."

"Lots of high school boys have after school jobs," Lu said helpfully.

"What I'm after right now is a job delivering the newspapers," Hogie said, squinting at the street lamp.

"That sounds wonderful!" said Lu.

"The only way I can get in is to be a substitute first. That's what I'm working on now. I'm supposed to get my answer Monday."

"I'm sure you'll get it," she said.

They walked along. Lu looked up at the sprinkle of stars. "It's pretty tonight," she said, "and quiet. It's nice walking like this."

"Most girls I've known hate walking. They like fellows to have cars." He kicked a bottle cap out of his path.

Lu said, "I like to walk."

Hogie turned to look at her. "You're different," he said.

"How different?" She made a face at him.

"The girls I've always run around with weren't a bit like you."

Lu glanced at him feeling uncertain. It always

made her feel uncomfortable, somehow, when Hogie spoke of other girls he had known. She wished he wouldn't. She frowned.

"I've never known a girl like you," he said.

Lu's frown slipped away magically.

They walked home in the chill evening, their hands clasped. When they reached the white house with the green shutters and the hawthorn crowding the porch, he kissed her.

"Goodnight," Lu whispered with a sigh. She watched him out of sight before she opened the door. Never in her dreams had she imagined a kiss like that.

10

"D<small>ID</small> <small>YOU</small> have a good time last night?" Charlotte asked. They sat on Lu's bed. It was Saturday morning. Only twelve hours after the night before. Lu smiled the soft private smile which she had awakened with, which hadn't come off when she had washed her face.

Lu stared out the window. The clouds lay in the sky too heavy to drift. Hogie was right, she reflected. The sky was seldom without clouds in Seattle. Even when the sky was blue, there were bunches of clouds.

"We walked," she said dreamily. "We left the game early and just walked."

"You *walked!*" said Charlotte.

"Hogie didn't have his car." Lu turned from her inspection of the world outside to her room. She half closed her eyes, noting how the room held a golden light even though the sun was not shining into it. "That's why he was late. He can't drive for a month."

Charlotte sat up. "You mean he *lost* his license!"

"It wasn't his fault," said Lu, opening her eyes wide.

"It must have been his fault, if he lost his license,"

Charlotte said. "Licenses aren't revoked for nothing."

"He didn't mean to go through a red light," Lu
said. "He didn't even know the light was there! It
wasn't really fair to take away his license on a little
thing like that!"

"It's a strict rule," said Charlotte. "If it's a moving
violation and a teen-aged driver, they automatically
take away his license no matter how minor it is."

"That doesn't make it fair!" said Lu.

Charlotte shrugged. Lu bent down to pick up a pin
from the floor. Her face felt hot, and she was an-
noyed suddenly with Charlotte, sitting there so pi-
ously as if she were the judge herself.

She went to the window and opened it a little way,
letting the cool air touch her face. She heard her
father's voice, coming from the garage.

"Angie! I almost ran into your bike! Get it out of
the driveway. You hear me!"

Lu winced. Everybody in the neighborhood could
hear him, she reflected. But Angie didn't seem to be
at all disturbed by the loudness of his father's voice.

"Okay Pop," he said.

Lu watched Angie amble over and move his bike
to the side of the driveway, only a few feet from where
it had lain all morning.

Charlotte got off the bed and came to stand beside
Lu. She peered out the window. Lu looked and saw
William Allen swinging up the block. He carried a

shopping bag. Some wilted celery stalks hung over the top.

"I guess I'd better go home," Charlotte said, but she didn't move.

"You might as well stay," said Lu, feeling sorry for Charlotte. "He'll go home pretty soon."

Charlotte shook her head. "Not until he checks my records." She threw her hands up in the air. "Records! I've got to keep regular records — on a pig!"

Lu watched William turn into the yard next door.

Charlotte made a face. "He calls me *Charlie!*"

Lu had to smile. "Well, it's businesslike, and short for Charlotte."

Charlotte groaned. She went to the door, put her hand on the knob and turned, with a brooding face, to regard Lu.

"You just don't know how lucky you are!" she said. Opening the door, she ran down the stairs.

Lu looked at herself in the mirror. She guessed she was pretty lucky at that. Her glance fell on the half-finished report on the desk behind her. It had been due in Miss Egbert's class on Friday. Lucky in love, anyway, she decided. And she smiled at her own face in the mirror.

She picked up the report and tried to put her mind on it. Hearing the kitchen door slam, a few minutes later, she raised her head, listening to Angie's running steps up the stairs. Lu went to the door. Angie was already going back down the hallway with a hot-water bottle in his hand.

"What's going on?" asked Lu.

Angie didn't stop. "He's sick," he said. He started down the stairs.

"Who?" shouted Lu over the railing.

Angie stopped a moment in the middle of the stairs. "Charlotte's pig. He ate something that disagreed with him, and now he won't eat anything."

Lu ran down after Angie. William Allen sat cross-legged before the pigpen.

"Nice pig," he cooed, "nice little pig." In his hand was a spoon and in the spoon was what looked like chocolate syrup.

"Maybe he doesn't like chocolate," Charlotte said, hovering over the pen.

"Pigs like everything," William said dryly. "It doesn't make any difference to them. They'll even eat broken glass, if it happens to be mixed with their food."

Charlotte gasped. "You didn't give him anything like *that,* did you!" Her voice was accusing.

William glanced at her briefly. "*I* didn't give him anything today," he said. "Remember, you fed him, today and yesterday."

Charlotte looked apologetic. "Well, I didn't feed him any broken glass," she said. "I gave him some leftover popcorn and a peanut butter sandwich I didn't eat for my lunch, and some rutabagas left over from last night's dinner that we were supposed to have for dinner tonight." She smiled fleetingly, and went on. "He had rye bread toast for breakfast and some orange peels."

"And some cooked oatmeal," put in Angie. "I brought that over myself," he said.

"That was supposed to be *your* breakfast," Lu pointed out.

"I figured why be stingy?" said Angie and grinned.

William's glance swept over them all.

"I didn't feed him anything," Lu said.

"What are we going to do?" said Charlotte. "He'll die if he doesn't eat."

William's lips spread into a thin smile. "He's at least five pounds heavier than when we got him. I'd say there's not much chance of his dying of starvation, anyway. We'll be lucky if he doesn't get too fat for this little pen before the Trade Fair."

"Some pigs get to be over a thousand pounds in no time at all," said Angie. "I looked it up in the encyclopedia. They grow awfully fast."

Charlotte threw a worried look at the flimsy pen. "If he grows much bigger, he'll look crated, instead of penned."

Lu giggled. "You're lucky I didn't suggest getting an elephant," she said. "They start at two thousand pounds."

Charlotte looked at her without smiling. "We'll

be lucky if we're not sued for killing the pig," she said.

William stood up. "If we could only find out what he ate — if he ate something strange, that is," he said. He turned to Charlotte. "Have you got your records up to date?"

"Of course," Charlotte said haughtily. "That's what I was supposed to do, wasn't I?"

She went into the house and returned with her school notebook. She leafed through it, came to the end, and started again, turning the pages more slowly. She frowned.

Patiently William Allen waited. "What's this?" he asked. He picked up a large clamp tied to the side of the pen.

Charlotte closed her notebook with a bang. "Oh, I forgot," she said. "Just this morning I put all the records together and clamped them to the pen. I thought it would be more convenient — " she stopped, and stared at the empty clamp hanging from the side of the pen. "Where are they?"

William Allen looked at her, at the empty clamp, then at the pig. He took a big bottle out of his back pocket, unscrewed the top, picked up the spoon, and remarked, "I think we'd better give him another spoonful of this chocolate-flavored laxative."

"You mean the pig ate the records?" shouted Angie.

Lu said, "No wonder he's got a stomachache."

"Gee William, I'm sorry," Charlotte said. "That was stupid of me. I know it was." She looked as if she were going to cry.

William turned his back. "At least we know what he ate," he said. "It was only paper. He'll be all right when he digests it." William recapped the bottle and tucked it again into his back pocket. "I'll look in on him in the evening," he said cheerfully, and made his way out of the yard and down the street.

Lu patted Charlotte's shoulder. "It's nothing to cry about," she said.

Charlotte took her hands away from her face. "I'm not crying," she said. "I'm trying to keep from laughing."

They looked at each other then, and they both laughed. They threw their arms around each other and shrieked.

Angie stood off, watching them with an expression of wonder.

"I don't see what's so funny," he said, and in imitation of William he turned his back and walked away.

I I

Lu smiled to herself as she slipped into Miss Egbert's room before class the next morning. The smile was for William Allen and Charlotte and the pig. The pig had slept soundly throughout the night and had awakened both families at dawn with his snorting and squealing for his breakfast. It was a story that would make Hogie laugh.

"What's this?" asked Miss Egbert. She picked up the neatly bound report which Lu had just laid on her desk, and flipped it open.

"My report," said Lu. "It was due Friday." Unhesitatingly she gave the teacher the whole truth — "I didn't finish it until last night."

Miss Egbert set it down on her desk. "Sit down a moment, Lu." She indicated the chair beside her desk. Lu sat down while Miss Egbert went over to the room door, unhooked the doorstop and shut the door.

"I've been meaning to talk to you," she explained, coming back and sitting down at her desk.

Lu wondered whether her mother had talked to Miss Egbert again. She waited politely. But Miss Egbert seemed in no hurry to begin. She glanced

79

through Lu's report, turning the pages slowly, making a mark or two in the middle of each page. She reached the last page, looked on as if she expected to see another one, and then turned the report face down.

"Adequate," she said. And spread out her hands. "No more — no less."

Under the teacher's gaze, Lu flushed.

"I have gone to some little trouble to check your previous grades. Your record is good," she said. "You have consistently been a better than average student. A little weak in math — but strong always in Language Arts." She leaned toward Lu and asked brusquely, "What happened?"

Lu was taken aback. "Why nothing, I guess. Nothing special, I mean."

Miss Egbert sat back. "When you first came into this class you daydreamed — " she said. "You stared out the window and you dreamed."

Lu's glance strayed to the window. A fine shower of rain had sprinkled the outside of the glass. She turned her head back to Miss Egbert.

"Of late," said Miss Egbert, "your attention has been inside the room — but it has not been on your work."

Lu fixed her glance on the edge of the teacher's desk where the sunlight silvered the corner.

Miss Egbert folded her hands and looked earnestly

at Lu. "It's always been my opinion that when a girl's grades drop, most often it's due to a boy."

Lu looked up.

Miss Egbert, too, straightened up. She had come, Lu knew, to the reason for this talk with her.

Miss Egbert said carefully, "Robert Hogan." She added cheerfully — "He's a very attractive boy in some ways."

Lu held her head up. Miss Egbert didn't understand him, not as she did. "Yes," she said.

"I think I should tell you that his school record has been deplorable. He has attended at least six schools in the last five years."

"I know," said Lu, pleased not to act surprised. "His father's work keeps the family traveling."

Miss Egbert looked at her gravely. "His father's method of coping with the rent is to move to another part of the city — and thus to another school."

A picture of Hogie's father yelling at the landlord rushed to her mind. "That's not his fault!" said Lu. It wasn't fair, she thought. It really wasn't fair.

Miss Egbert pursed her lips. "No, I suppose not," she said. "But I also happen to know that he left some debts of his own. His last school is still holding his credits until he pays for books lost or not returned."

Lu smiled. "He's getting a job," she said. "He's taking a paper route." She raised her chin. "He'll pay off every penny he owes."

Miss Egbert regarded her. Softly she said, "I hope you're right."

The classroom door burst open then and a few students bounded in. Lu made her way to her seat. There was no time to talk privately with Hogie, for he was late coming to class, and Miss Egbert called him in during the noon hour to reprimand him about not turning in his report. It wasn't until school was over that Lu was able to meet him and talk with him.

"Did you get the job?" she asked anxiously.

He smiled at her slowly, his eyes lighting up as they always did when he gazed at her.

"Well — yes and no," he drawled.

She threw him a puzzled look.

"I got a temporary job," he said. "I'm taking a fellow's place who broke his arm. It's only for a month — to start with."

Lu breathed a sigh of relief. Surely in a month's time Hogie would be able to earn enough to pay off whatever he owed.

"Come on," he said, taking her books and piling them upon his own. "I'll treat you to a Coke."

She fell into step beside him. He would have to save every penny, she decided, and she would have to do what she could to help him.

"I'll treat," she said, feeling virtuous.

He stopped, and surprised at the swift action, she stopped too.

He faced her with a tight look. "When I take you out, I pay!" he said. "Get me?"

Her heart pounded suddenly as she saw the fierceness in his eyes, and then understanding melted her resolve. She had hurt his pride! She should have remembered he had tremendous pride.

"I meant just until you get paid," she amended.

The smile came to his eyes again. "You're sweet," he whispered, and as someone jostled them in passing, he took her arm. "But don't you waste any time worrying about me," he said. "I can take care of myself."

"I know you can," she said promptly.

They walked along, close together.

"I'm taking over this Sunday," he said. He grimaced. "Four o'clock! The only catch is to wake up at that awful hour." His smile was rueful. "I sleep like a log."

"I'll call you!" she said, eager to make up for her mistake. "The telephone is right outside my bedroom door and I'll set my alarm and wake you, promptly at four!"

He looked at her with appreciation. "Good enough," he said. "Let it ring until I answer. Nothing could wake my dad."

She nodded, and together they walked into the Coke shop.

12

Lu closed the door of her room and spread out her books on the bed. Feeling full of good intentions, she picked up her language arts book and checked the page assignment in her notebook. She began to read. At the bottom of the third page she recalled the fierce look Hogie had given her when she had offered to help by treating, and she went back and read the paragraph again with a warm feeling in her heart.

It would be terrible if no one believed in you, she reflected, and felt sorry for Hogie, yanked out of school and placed in another every year or so. No wonder he had never had any real friends.

He needs me, she thought, and his need made her feel sure and wise. No one had ever really needed her before. His brashness was a cover-up, she perceived. And suddenly, she admired him anew, for being loyal to his father, for speaking of him proudly, as if he were just like anybody's father. Like her own, for instance.

Lu tried to think what it would be like to be sorry for her father — but the feeling was unimaginable.

It had never occurred to her how lucky she was to have a father like hers.

She focused on the words on the page before her, and read the paragraph again.

It was strange how she and Hogie had been drawn together, she thought. Perhaps it was fate, Hogie was her fate, she decided, and wondered, all at once, what the meaning of the word really was. On impulse, she turned her book face down and slid off the bed. The dictionary was not on the pile of books on her desk. She opened the bedroom door.

"Angie!" she called. Angie's door was wide open. She went across the hall and looked in. There was no dictionary on the shelf next to his bird's nest. A half-dozen volumes of the *World Book* were scattered over his bed; a pile of astronomy magazines lay on the floor. A Sears Roebuck catalogue open to the page of telescopes was the only book on his desk.

Lu ran downstairs. "Anybody see the dictionary?" she said, bursting into the kitchen.

"Studying?" her father said, and his smile was like a pat on the head. He went back to the work he was doing on the kitchen table.

Her mother said, "Angie had it in the living room last night."

Lu went into the living room, found the book under a pile of magazines and carried it upstairs.

"Did you find it?" her mother called up after her in a helpful tone of voice.

Lu paused before her bedroom door. "I've got it!" she called back. Before closing the door, she heard her mother say to her father — "It could even be the first step to being erudite."

She carried the book back to her bed. She wondered what *erudite* meant, and looked up *fate*.

"Destiny," she read. "Something inevitable." She nodded, pleased, and read on. "Death, destruction, doom." She flapped the book closed and frowned.

There was a light tapping at the door. "Come in," she called.

Her mother stood in the doorway. "Your father said he had a Webster's College Dictionary down at his office and — "

"Thanks," said Lu. "I don't need it."

Her mother looked around the room. Lu gazed at her and could see that it was an effort for her to keep the smile on her face.

"I thought you were practically finished painting your room," her mother said.

Lu looked around. "It is, practically," she said.

Her mother shook herself a little. "One wall?"

Lu glanced at the gold wall, and then down at the cans of paint stacked in the corner. "I have to go down and exchange some gold paint for some white," she said. "Maybe I'll do that today."

"Finish your schoolwork first," her mother said.

"I will," said Lu. She waited until her mother had gone out, and closed the door behind her.

She picked up the language arts book again, and started to read. But the words didn't make sense to her — no sense at all. She checked back in her notebook for the assignment, and looked at the page number of the book. She smiled at herself. No wonder the words didn't make sense — she had been reading the wrong chapter.

She settled herself against her pillows and started over again.

A loud shout awakened her. She jumped up. The book, which had been pressed against her chest, slipped to the floor.

"Lu!" It was Angie.

Lu opened the bedroom door.

"Time for dinner!" he hollered.

Lu rubbed her eyes and looked at the watch on her wrist. But it was too dark to see what time it was. "I'll be right down," she called, and went to wash her face.

Her mother and father turned to her with expectant looks as she sat down. "Well!" said her father, "how did it go?"

"Fine," she said, not looking at him.

"You'll have plenty of time to finish your painting next Saturday," said her mother.

Lu had forgotten all about exchanging the paint.

"What are you doing now in Miss Egbert's class?" her mother asked with interest.

Lu tried to remember what the chapter had been

about, and couldn't recall it. "We just turned in a report," she said.

"Fine teacher, that Miss Egbert," said her father. "Seems to think a lot of you, Lu."

Lu looked at her father.

"Thinks you are capable of doing a lot more than you are doing."

Lu made a face. "She thinks everybody is capable of doing more than anybody is doing."

Her father laughed, appreciating her words. "Well, I suppose that's true enough," he said.

"What are you doing, Angie?" Lu was glad that her mother had turned her attention to Angie.

"Pigs like corn," Angie said, measuring out creamed corn into two sauce dishes.

"So do I," said his father, and picking up the second dish he set it before him and began to eat.

"You can give the pig what's left over," said his mother.

Angie eyed his father. "Doesn't look like there's going to be anything left over the way some people eat around here," he said.

His father ignored him. "Delicious lamb chops," he murmured. "Have one, Angie."

Angie allowed a chop to be put on his plate.

"There won't be any leftover chops," his mother warned. "Not at these prices."

Lu said, "The pig doesn't really care what he eats,

Angie. It's all one and the same to him."

"It'll probably be dead by the time the Trade Fair starts," said Angie. "The way it gets fed around here."

"Eat your dinner, Angie," said his father.

"I don't know why you're so worried about that pig of Charlotte's anyway," said Mrs. Martin. "It isn't your concern."

"But we are concerned — in a way," Mr. Martin announced. The three stared at him. "That is, we have an interest in it," he qualified. "Three shares' worth to be exact."

It had never occurred to Lu to sell stock to her own father. She wondered if Charlotte . . .

"Sound investment!" Mr. Martin made it sound like a proclamation. "A boy named William Allen sold me. A fine lad! He pointed out that my own bank recommends them highly. It happens to be one of the counseling firms."

Mrs. Martin gave him a little smile and Lu smiled, too, because it was just like William.

"Is it a lot of money?" Angie asked, much impressed.

"Three shares, 50¢ a share, a total of $1.50."

"I don't suppose we will lose much on that investment even if the company goes bankrupt," Mrs. Martin said.

"They won't go bankrupt," said Angie, in that important voice Lu noticed he used whenever he spoke of money. "William Allen said they've already cut out dozens of cutting boards. All they have to do is sell them. They'll make plenty!" Envy was there in his voice.

"We don't get to use the profits, though," said Lu, and she couldn't help grinning. She guessed he was thinking about his telescope. "It all goes back into the Junior Achievement company. Whatever extra is made is paid out in dividends."

"The pig is going to be a big success at the Trade Fair," said Angie with bright confidence. "He's going to bring in lots of customers."

It was her idea, Lu reflected with satisfaction.

"It's a fine project," Mr. Martin said. "I think young people should learn about business."

Lu said, not hiding her pride, "Hogie has a job now. He'll be delivering *The Seattle Times* starting tomorrow morning."

It was still dark outside when Lu's alarm whirred. She sat up and turned it off. Then she put on her bathrobe and slippers and went out into the dark hallway. The flick of the light switch seemed to make a loud noise in the quiet hallway.

She yawned as she dialed Hogie's number. It rang three times before it was answered, sleepily, by a gruff voice.

"Who's that?" the voice said.

Lu swallowed her smile. The ring must have awakened Hogie's father. "May I speak to Hogie, please?"

"Hogie?" he said foggily. Then she heard a mumble and a rasp, and finally Hogie's "Hello?"

"Time to get up!" she said.

He groaned.

Her laugh was an indulgent one.

"It's still dark outside!"

"Of course, silly. It's only four o'clock."

His groan came again louder, longer.

Angie's door opened. He stood there in his doorway, tousled, sleepy-eyed, his pajamas hanging loosely on his skinny body.

"Whatsa matter?" he said and yawned.

Lu put her hand over the mouthpiece. "Go back to bed," she said, "I'm just waking up Hogie for his paper route."

Angie became wide awake instantly. "Hey! Ask him if I can help him. Will you? Will you ask him if I can go the rounds with him?"

Lu made a face at his intensity. She said over the telephone, "Angie wants to know whether he can go with you?"

"Sure," Hogie said. "Why not? Tell him to start folding the papers if he gets there before I do."

"He'll meet you at the news shack," Lu told Angie, as she hung up.

"Oh boy!" said Angie, pulling his pajama top over his head as he dashed into his room.

Lu smiled. It was nice of Hogie to let Angie go along, she thought. She yawned then, and made her way back to her warm bed.

13

THE SMELL of baking waffles and bubbling coffee greeted Lu as she came downstairs hours later. She yawned luxuriously and entered the kitchen.

"Good morning," her father said.

Her mother said, "I wonder what's keeping Angie in bed so long."

"Oh, he's not in bed," said Lu. "He got up early to help Hogie deliver his papers. He just wanted to go along," she said comfortably.

"Good experience," said her father, turning the Sunday newspaper around and creasing it so he could read while sipping his coffee.

The kitchen door opened. "Am I hungry!" said Angie. He came in, dropped his jacket on a chair, and sat down at the table.

"Your hands," his mother reminded him. "And your face could do with a washing, too."

Angie pushed his chair back. "It's the fresh ink," he said importantly. "The papers are hardly dry when they come to the shack. You can't help getting smudgy when you fold them."

He went out, and came back a moment later with

his hands scrubbed, but still gray. He held them out, looking at them with satisfaction. "Probably won't ever come off," he said.

He sat down at the table and poured syrup over his waffles. "It won't take us so long next time," he remarked, "because now we know the route."

"What do you mean *we?*" said Lu.

"Hogie doesn't mind if I help him," Angie said. "He says he might even pay me for my trouble."

Lu put down her fork. "Pay you!"

Angie shrugged. "Sure, why not? Lots of guys divide up with helpers. And if they're sick or something, the helper knows the route and can take it."

"But Hogie doesn't need a helper," said Lu, and her voice was louder than she meant it to be.

Her father looked at her.

"Why not?" said Angie.

"He's just a substitute himself, remember?"

Angie nodded. "I'm the substitute's substitute, then," he said.

Mr. Martin laughed. "Sounds like overspecialization to me."

"Beats selling greeting cards, any day," said Angie, gulping his milk. "I figure this will put me over the hump — if I can help every Sunday for a month."

"I wouldn't count on it if I were you," Lu warned. "After all Hogie wants to earn the money himself."

Angie was undaunted. "He'll want me to help

96

him," he declared. "Just wait and see. He'll want me."

"It was nice of you to offer to pay Angie for going with you, Sunday," Lu said, choosing her words as if she were stepping over cracks on the sidewalk. They left the school building together.

"He's a good kid," said Hogie.

She abandoned the game and said, "You don't have to let him help you, Hogie. I mean — don't let him be a nuisance about it."

But he misunderstood her. "Oh, he's not a nuisance. He's a pretty good little helper. He's getting a real kick out of it."

Lu was silent. She remembered how sensitive Hogie was about money. She decided she couldn't really come out and remind him that he needed everything he could earn on the route himself. Lu sighed.

He took her arm. "Things are going to be different for me from now on," he said.

"I know it," she said warmly, and was ashamed of herself for her doubts.

He tilted his head and examined the thick grey sky. "I'll be seventeen next Saturday."

"Your birthday!" she said, and wondered what she could give him for a present.

"May I borrow your pen a moment?" she asked.

97

He pulled one from the pocket of his shirt and handed it to her. She was disappointed to see that it was a good one, better than hers, and crossed that possibility off her mind. She opened her notebook and wrote the date boldly across a blank sheet, and handed the pen back to him. She wished she had known about his birthday earlier.

"What size shoe do you wear?" she asked.

"You want to borrow my shoes?"

She giggled. "No, but I was thinking about knitting you a pair of socks. Once I knitted a pair for my father for Christmas." She thought of them. "I don't think he ever got around to wearing them, though. We used them as Santa stockings, and he always claimed we left nuts in the toes." She chuckled. "I guess I'd better not knit you any socks," she said.

"You can give me your picture," he suggested.

She tried not to smile. "Okay. Which one do you want: the one of me sitting on a pony, or the one I had taken a little later — at my tenth birthday party?"

"On second thought, don't bother," he said. "I've got a picture of you already."

"You haven't!" She wondered whether he really did have.

He tapped his forehead. "Right here, up in my head."

She felt inordinately pleased.

She walked with him all the way to the news shack. The truck carrying the evening edition arrived as they got there and she crossed the street and stood watching a moment as the boys scrambled onto it and threw off the bundles of papers. Then she turned away and walked up the street thinking about Hogie's birthday. It began to rain then, and she walked in the rain smiling.

She tried to think of something significant to give Hogie for his birthday. Something really significant. Nothing came to mind.

She looked hopefully into the store windows as she passed them, and saw nothing really significant that would do. A gust of wind hit her face as she turned the corner, and she stepped into the entrance of a store to pull out her scarf and tie it around her head. Then she went into the shop.

"I'm looking for a birthday present — for somebody," she said to the girl standing behind the counter. She picked up a man's leather-backed brush and put it down again.

"Handkerchiefs?" asked the salesgirl.

Lu shook her head.

"You can't go wrong on a tie," the girl told her.

"No," Lu said frowning. It was a mistake to have asked.

"Tie clip? Cuff Links? Gloves?"

Obediently Lu bent to look at the pair of gloves displayed in the glass case. "I'm looking for something — well, special," she explained, not really seeing them.

The saleswoman said, "These are all very special, I'd say."

Lu shook her head. "Something significant — I mean."

"How much do you want to spend?" asked the saleswoman.

Lu gave a little shrug. The truth was she wasn't sure how much. She would have to ask her father for an advance on next month's allowance. "Maybe I'd better look around a bit more," she said.

She walked quickly down the long counter away from the saleswoman. Ahead of her was an aisle counter displaying billfolds.

Lu stopped. A wallet! That's what she would get. The significance of it impressed her. She whirled about and went back to the saleswoman.

"How much are the wallets over there?" she asked.

The woman didn't even look up. "They're marked," she said, turning to put some boxes upon the shelf.

Lu went back to the display counter. She picked up a wallet and looked inside: $5.95. She put it down and looked at another. It was marked $2.95. Quickly she looked through a few more. The prices varied.

A white-haired salesman smiled at her from the other end of the counter. "Genuine pigskin," he said. "A real buy."

"I'll be back," she said. "This is just what I want. Just exactly. I'll be back tomorrow to get one."

Reaching home, she waited for her father to arrive.

100

And then she decided to wait until after dinner to ask him. All the while she scraped the dinner dishes, rinsed them, and stacked them into the dishwasher, she thought about the gift for Hogie. Angie finished his job of bringing the dishes in from the dining room and went upstairs. Mrs. Martin always put away the leftover food, but it was Angie's job to clear the table every night, and Lu's to get the dishes into the dishwasher. Lu looked into the dining room and saw that Angie had left the salt and pepper shakers on the table.

"Angie," she shouted.

"What d'you want!" yelled Angie from the second floor hall.

"You didn't finish your job!"

Angie came down, picked up the salt and pepper shakers, plopped them on the kitchen counter, and went upstairs again. Lu had to move them to wipe off the counter, and she set them out of her way, back on the dining-room table. But she wasn't thinking of them, particularly, she was thinking of the wallet which she wanted to buy as a gift for Hogie. She needed $2. That's all she needed. It wasn't very much to spend for a wallet, but what counted, she decided, was the significance of the gift.

She had it already wrapped and tied with a ribbon in her mind when she approached her father for the advance.

"It's for something very special," she said, hoping

he wouldn't ask what was so special. But she needn't have worried, for he didn't.

He said, "I've already given you an advance on your next month's allowance."

Lu remembered then. He had given her some extra money to buy the paint. "Oh," she said. She stood there a moment watching him as he turned the pages of the newspaper. He glanced up, frowned, and she turned away.

In the kitchen her mother was taking the dishes out of the dishwasher and setting them in the cupboard. Helpfully Lu picked up a dish and held it. Her mother looked at her.

"Will you lend me a couple of dollars, Mother?" she asked, setting down the dish again.

Her mother picked up the dish and placed it where it belonged in the cupboard. She frowned, but whether at the dish or Lu's request, Lu did not know. Mrs. Martin wouldn't approve of her buying a gift for Hogie, she knew, and she did not offer an explanation.

"Your allowance was supposed to cover all your miscellaneous expenses," her mother pointed out.

Lu waited.

"Whatever it is you want, I think it had better come out of your regular allowance," her mother said.

Lu went into the living room, through it, and up the stairs. Angie was sitting on the top step.

"What do you want the $2 for?" he asked.

Lu stepped over his feet. "It's Hogie's birthday," she said. "I want to buy him a birthday present." Wistfully, she added, "A wallet."

"I don't mind lending you a couple of dollars," Angie said.

She stopped and turned around.

"It's part of the money for my telescope," he said. "But if you're sure you'll pay it back when I need it, you can have it — for Hogie."

"I'll pay it back out of my next allowance," she promised.

She followed him into his room and stood back while he opened his drawer and counted out two dollars in nickels and dimes and pennies. He poured the amount into her cupped hands.

"He's a pretty good guy, that Hogie," Angie said.

Lu looked at the handful of money. "I know it," she said, and turned happily toward her room.

14

L<small>U</small> LEANED over the pen and inspected the pig.

"I scrubbed him," Charlotte said. "Won't he look beautiful today in our booth at the Trade Fair?"

"Beautiful," agreed Lu. But she wasn't thinking of the pig. She was thinking of the wallet, gift-wrapped and waiting. The day was Hogie's birthday.

Charlotte said, "I never thought I'd ever play nursemaid to a pig. That William!"

Lu thought of William. He had none of Hogie's unpredictable sense of fun. She continued to think of Hogie.

"He's gone to borrow a truck," Charlotte told her. "We have to take the pig to the Trade Fair early this morning."

"Hogie and I are on the second shift," Lu reminded her, thinking of Hogie's delight when she would give him the birthday present.

With an effort Lu brought her mind back. "My mother thinks the boards are cute," said Lu. "She's going to buy one."

"My mother won't," said Charlotte. "She says she's sick of pigs and anything that looks like one." Charlotte smiled. "She doesn't know it but she's getting a complimentary sample of the cutting board. William carved her name on it."

"The truck's here!" shouted Angie. He raced around from the front street.

William came, striding, after him. He nodded at Lu. "We're going to move the whole thing," he said to Charlotte. "I've got a couple of fellows with me. We're going to put the pigpen and all right on the truck and slide it off right at the spot we want it."

"How do you think he looks?" said Charlotte.

William glanced at the pig. "He hasn't been eating any more reports, has he?" he said, worry in his voice.

"Of course not!" said Charlotte. "I washed and brushed him." She looked at the animal with pride.

"Oh!" said William. "Maybe that's why he looks so strange." He turned his back and shouted to the boys out front. "He's ready!"

Lu patted Charlotte's arm. They watched the boys load the pig and his pen onto the truck. Then the two helpers scrambled onto the back of the truck and steadied the crate.

"You coming?" said William, holding the cab door open.

Charlotte looked at Lu, and moved to board the cab.

"I'll see you later!" Lu called as the truck moved down the street.

Hogie walked along beside her with his hands stuck in his back pockets. The green hat sat, tipped, on his head.

Feeling the wallet in her pocket, she gave a little skip. "I've got something for you. A birthday present." She drew it out.

He stopped walking in surprise. "You really did get something for me?"

"Of course," she said. "Open it."

He pulled weakly at the bow.

"Not that way, silly, just slip it off." She stretched over to help him, and he raised it, holding it out of her reach.

"Whose birthday is this, anyway?"

She smiled as he removed the bow and turned the wallet over and over in his hands.

"Thanks," he said. "Thanks a lot. I mean, you shouldn't have done it — "

"You're supposed to say — 'it's just what I needed!' " she said, hoping he got the significance of it.

"It's just what I needed," he said — "if you say so."

She laughed, and steered him across the street and to the entrance of the shopping center. A banner flapped over their heads.

"Junior Achievement Trade Fair," Hogie spelled out.

They went from store to store looking for their own company. Junior Achievement booths were set up inside many of the stores. Some of the booths lined the mall.

In front of the beauty salon, Charlotte waved to Lu.

"We're right next door," she said. "It was an empty store, and because of the pig, they let us have it."

Lu and Hogie looked through the plate-glass window. A long counter had been set up at which the pig-shaped cutting boards were being demonstrated and displayed. The pigpen was set in the middle of the floor. Children pushed and shoved around the pen to get closer to the little bristling pink and black animal.

William Allen came striding up, his face shiny with worry. He hardly saw Lu and Hogie. "They're smothering the pig with attention," he said. "We've got to get it in a more protected position."

"Why don't we put the pen against the big window," Charlotte said. "Half the kids could look at him through the window, from the outside."

William Allen clapped her on the back. "Good thinking, Charlie!" he said, while Lu turned away to smile.

"Come on," said Charlotte. "Help me get these kids out of the way." Lu followed Charlotte.

"This way, please," Charlotte shouted.

"Will you please move back?" Lu said softly to the knot of youngsters hanging over the pen. And Hogie grinned and shouted, "Grandstand seats at the window!"

Lu watched him. He knew exactly how to handle people. He grinned at the kids and the kids grinned back at him — and moved.

As the children filed out, William Allen and another boy and Hogie began to shift the position of the pen.

Lu and Charlotte stood at the open door, keeping the children out as the pen moved past them to the big window.

"Heave ho!" said Hogie, helping to push the pen along.

And suddenly there was a squeal and a grunt and the pen collapsed. Lu had a fleeting impression of Hogie's face caught in surprise, and the next moment the pig ran past her and out into the mall.

Charlotte screamed. And William made a dash out the door after the small animal. The pig grunted and squealed and snorted loudly as it darted from one pair of legs to another.

"Catch him!" shouted Charlotte. "Somebody catch him!"

But the people on the mall were frightened of the lunging animal and they all jumped back. The pig streaked through the crowd, turned the corner and disappeared.

For an instant they stood there looking at each other.

"We're responsible," said William hoarsely.

"We're completely responsible for everything the pig does."

Lu swallowed the lump in her throat. In a way, she was more responsible than anyone. It was her idea, wasn't it?

"We'll go through all the stores on this side," Charlotte said to William as she grabbed Lu's hand. "You go the other way."

"I'll stick around here," said Hogie, "in case you flush him back."

Lu followed Charlotte.

"He could be anywhere!" said Charlotte waving her arms around, and walking fast. They went around the corner and turned into the first store. It was a hardware store.

"We're looking for a pig," Charlotte said to the man at the cash register. The man wore a white shirt and tie. His face was round and his ears made him look rounder. He was adding up figures that were marked on a little tape at the side of the machine. He motioned with the end of his pencil, over his shoulder.

"The butcher shop is up the street," he said.

Lu gasped.

Charlotte said clearly, "The pig we're looking for has escaped — I mean run away."

The man put his pencil down on the desk and looked at the two girls. Then he put his hand to his mouth and bawled in the direction of the back room. "Has anybody seen these girls' pig?"

An old lady standing at the card sample counter turned around. "My, my," she said. "What strange pets children have nowadays."

Lu pulled Charlotte out.

They walked up the street. A man was sweeping the walk in front of the moving picture theater. The doors were wide open. They stopped and looked at each other, and then went up to the man.

"This show doesn't start until 2:30 P.M.," he said, not stopping his sweeping.

"We don't want to go to the show," said Charlotte. "We just want to ask you about a pig."

He stopped sweeping. "We don't allow any pigs," he said, and went on sweeping.

"Come on, Charlotte," said Lu, but she couldn't help giggling.

They looked into every shop on that side of the mall, and went through the department store to the other side. William Allen waved to them from the other entrance. They hurried over to where he stood.

"He's behind the candy counter," William whispered. "Only the girl doesn't know it."

"May I help you?" the candy girl said. She smiled. "We have a special on — " she stopped. Her mouth opened and closed and her eyes grew round. "Y-urrr!" she said and ran out from behind the counter.

William dashed in and the pig lunged out. He slithered across the polished floor snorting and squealing and ran out the doorway. William Allen sprang after it and Lu and Charlotte ran after him.

The beauty salon door swung open, and just before it closed again, the pig plunged in.

William looked at Charlotte and Charlotte looked at Lu. They groaned, all together.

"You'd better go in and get it," said William to Charlotte.

"Me!" shrieked Charlotte.

William looked at her a moment, then strode to the door of the beauty shop. He opened it, and it closed behind him.

A few moments later William emerged. He carried the pig, snorting and squealing, by its hind legs. William's ears, Lu reflected, were as pink as the stripe on the pig's back.

Charlotte ran to William. "I'll hold him," she offered bravely, "until you put the pen together again."

"That's okay," he said. "We'll lock him in the storeroom until we can get his pen fixed."

Charlotte heaved a sigh of relief.

In retrospect it seemed even funnier. Lu and Hogie reviewed the incident in laughter again and again on their way home.

Angie stood on the porch watching them curiously as they came down the street.

"Hi Hogie!" Angie called. "You want me to help you deliver the papers tomorrow?"

Lu frowned at him.

Hogie shrugged. "It's up to you, kid," he said.

"Okay," said Angie. He grinned triumphantly at Lu.

Lu said goodbye to Hogie at the porch steps.

"I'd stick around, but I've got to do some newspaper collecting this afternoon."

Angie came closer. "I'll collect for you, Hogie. You want me to collect for you?"

Hogie grinned at Lu and winked. "Say, the little brother is turning into quite a businessman. No thanks, Angie," he said, giving him an affectionate sock on the arm. "I'll do my own collecting, if you don't mind."

Lu smiled back at Hogie. Her concern had been only her imagination. Hogie was as anxious as she that he earn all he could on this job.

15

At five o'clock, the telephone rang.

"Hey!" said Hogie. "How would you like to go bowling? I have some free tickets."

Lu looked over her shoulder. "Just a minute," she said and placed the receiver down.

Her mother was sweeping the porch. She wore jeans and her husband's old fishing jacket. Her hair was flying about in the breeze. Lu quickly looked up and down the block. She hoped no one would see her mother like that. She held the door open.

"I'm going bowling with Hogie tonight, that's all right, isn't it?"

Her mother didn't stop sweeping.

Lu said, "It's his birthday!"

Her mother leaned on the broom, looking at her.

"We won't be out late," said Lu. "Hogie has to get up early to deliver the papers."

Her mother nodded and Lu rushed back to the telephone.

"I did all my collecting today," Hogie said as they walked up the street. He tucked her hand into his pocket. "Seems to me we ought to celebrate a little."

Hogie hurried her across the street, and they boarded the bus that drew up there.

"Anyway, we won't have to ride the bus back," Hogie said, as he sat down beside her.

Lu looked at him in surprise.

"We're going to meet a fellow I know at the bowling alley. And his girl. He's been giving me a ride to school every morning."

The fellow he knew was Jim Haley, and Lu smiled at the basketball player with recognition.

"Hi," he said with a half wave, while Sandra Collins and Lu smiled at each other.

They played two games, and then the alley was so crowded they decided not to bowl anymore at all.

"I'm hungry," Sandra announced.

Jim regarded her fondly. "You're always hungry," he said. "If all the hamburgers I've bought for you were laid end to end, they'd choke a horse."

Sandra chuckled and put her arm through his. "We could go to the Burger Drive-In. They're cheap!"

"I'm hungry too," said Lu, thinking that hamburgers didn't really cost very much.

They drove over the Montlake Bridge, around the stadium, and past the garbage dump. They sang as they rode, Jim beating time for them by hitting the wheel of the car with his free hand. Suddenly Sandra stopped singing.

114

"You're going too fast, Jim," she said.

Jim speeded up a little, singing louder.

Sandra said more loudly, "Slow down! Jim. You're going too fast!"

Jim came to a sudden screeching halt. Lu, saved from a lurching tumble only by Hogie's firm arm, sat back, a little frightened.

"I didn't ask you to stop," said Sandra in an uncomfortable voice. "I just asked you to slow down."

Jim stared straight ahead, his foot quiet on the pedal, his hands unmoving on the wheel.

Suddenly Sandra laughed. "Come on, honey, I didn't mean to be such a — a — thing!" she said.

He turned his head then. "Okay," he said, and they moved slowly out into the middle of the road. Very slowly they moved along, so slowly that Lu looked quickly at Hogie and then at the back of Sandy's head. Sandy sat, her hands folded in her lap, her head held stiffly.

Suddenly Hogie chuckled. "Well, Jim old boy," he said, "now that we know who's boss, let's get going."

Sandra turned around. She was so pretty when she smiled, thought Lu, and smiled back.

"I'm sorry, Hogie," Sandra said. "It just makes me so mad when he goes fast."

The car resumed its normal speed. Jim turned and winked at them. "She scares easily, this girl does."

Sandra smiled. "Well, you always drive too fast."

They laughed a lot as they sat in the car and ate their hamburgers. Then they drove back around the wide arterial which edged the lake. The buildings on the University of Washington hilltop campus loomed over them.

"That's where I'm going when I finish high school," said Lu.

Jim scowled. "That's where I thought I was going," he said.

Sandra looked out the window on the opposite side. "I love the old garbage dump when the gulls fly over it," she said.

"I do, too," said Lu turning her head. "It's one of the most beautiful sights in Seattle."

Hogie groaned. "Listen to them," he implored Jim, "all that excitement about some crows over a dump."

"Not crows," said Lu, "gulls. They fly in from the bay. It's one of their favorite places. They sit on the roof of the pavilion building at the edge of the swampy area. That roof sometimes looks shingled with white gulls!"

Hogie snorted. "Scavengers," he said.

Sandra giggled. "It's all in the way you look at it, I guess."

A few minutes later, Jim stopped the car before

116

Lu's house. Hogie walked with her up to the front door while Jim and Sandra waited.

Lu said, "They're nice." She wondered what Charlotte would say when she told her that they had been double-dating with *seniors*.

"Jim's a good kid," Hogie said. "They were a little jumpy tonight because they just got married."

She looked at him in astonishment. "Married?"

"It's a secret," he said. "They ran off last weekend and got married."

Lu said, "She's pretty." Because she didn't know what to say. It had never occurred to her that getting married was as simple as that.

The car horn honked several short reminding toots.

"You'd better go," she said.

He kissed her then, quickly, and hard. Then he backed down the steps. "Goodnight."

"Goodnight," she said, staring back at him, and she watched him until he got into the car.

16

At four o'clock the next morning, Lu slipped out of bed and called Hogie. She smiled as she dialed the number.

A sleepy voice answered.

"Time to — " she began gaily.

"Okay — " said Hogie and hung up.

Tiptoeing so as not to wake Angie, Lu went back to bed. She lay there staring at the ceiling, her arms under her head, and her smile feeling tender on her face. And she closed her eyes, seeing Hogie's smile, and the way his eyebrows lifted in surprise, and how tall he was standing next to her.

She drifted off to sleep thinking about Hogie. But she dreamed about Jim. In her dream, Lu was Sandra, married to Jim, and they were driving in Hogie's car. "You're driving too fast!" she shouted at Jim, who was driving the wrong way down a one-way street. Only it wasn't Jim, all at once it was Hogie who was driving, and she wasn't Sandra anymore, she was Lu. "Slow down!" she shouted in her dream.

And then she woke up, lying stiffly on her back, her head slightly raised, listening, as if to a telephone bell which had pealed long ago. But all she heard was the sound of a door closing in the distance, and this too, she decided, must have been only part of the dream.

She thrust its remnants out of her mind, turned over, and went back to sleep.

"Good morning," she said gaily to her parents as she entered the kitchen. She poured a glass of orange juice from the pitcher and sniffed hungrily at the waffles in the iron. "What's keeping Angie?"

Her father turned the page of the newspaper. "He ought to be here in a moment," he said.

Her mother said, "I'm keeping some cooked oatmeal warm for him."

Lu set down her glass. "Where is he?" She was answered by a stamping at the back door. Angie's face appeared through the window glass. He came in, the paper boy's bag hanging emptily over him.

"I did the whole thing myself!" he said, pulling the empty bag over his head. He dropped it on the chair.

"Where was Hogie?" Lu said. Her voice sounded odd.

"He didn't get there until I was just about through," Angie said. "Lucky I was there," he said smugly. "One boy got fired because he showed up pretty late."

Lu looked at the orange juice in her glass, then

picked up the glass and drank.

"I guess I made a whole dollar today," said Angie, with satisfaction. "That's what the other fellows said. The regular boy pays over a dollar if you do the whole route for him."

"That's fine," said his father.

"Will you look through the catalogues with me today, Dad?" Angie's eagerness made him stutter. "I got a bunch of them the other day."

Lu pushed back her chair.

"You haven't finished your breakfast, Lu," her mother said.

Lu said, "I'm not very hungry." She ran up the stairs.

She lay on her bed, not thinking, listening to the murmur of voices from downstairs. Angie came pounding up, excitedly talking to his father right be-

hind him. Lu heard them go into Angie's room.

"You should see this one, Dad!" Angie was saying earnestly. "It's got a 2.4 inch refractor and two oculars. And a solar lens and a lunar lens. It magnifies up to 140 times!" His words fell over themselves. "This is the one I've been saving for."

"Hmmmm," Lu heard her father's low rumble. "You've got to have enough money to cover the postage, you know," he warned.

Lu turned over. Her father believed in a person's carrying a project right through to the end. He believed in being responsible. The tears that slid across her face into the corner of her mouth tasted bitter.

"The postage always comes collect," Angie said. "And I'll be able to take care of that all right. Lu is holding a couple of dollars for me."

The bed squeaked as her father rose from it in the other room.

"I figure I'll be able to mail the order this week," Angie's voice was filled with importance.

Hastily Lu wiped her face on the inside of her sweater.

She avoided Hogie at school the next day, pretending nothing was wrong. After school, Lu dropped her books on the bed and stood gazing out the window. Charlotte's back door slammed, and looking that way, Lu watched Charlotte slowly cross the yard to the pigpen.

Lu hastened out. "Hi," she said in the usual greeting. But her voice sounded thin.

Charlotte didn't seem to notice. "I thought you waited around to walk home with Hogie," Charlotte said.

"Not tonight," said Lu as if it had just happened that way.

Charlotte looked up. "What's the matter? You have a fight?"

Lu hesitated. "No. I guess you can call it a difference of opinion." She made a face. "He doesn't even know about it," she said.

Charlotte nodded. She leaned over the pen. "He's kind of cute, at that," she said, looking at the pig, and she sighed.

"Are you going to take him back to the farm today?" asked Lu.

Charlotte nodded. "William said he would. He said I didn't have to help if I didn't want to."

Lu looked at her closely. "You mean you want to?"

"Well, I guess I don't want to really, but it'll probably be the last time I'll see William."

"I thought you couldn't stand him!" said Lu.

Charlotte seemed not to have heard her. Leaning over the pig, she said dreamily, "I got to know him before I got to like him." She sighed. "He's the kind of boy you have to admire when you get to know him."

Lu regarded her friend thoughtfully.

"He calls me Charlie," she said. "It's his special name for me."

The pig grunted.

Lu thrust her hands into her pockets. "I know what you mean," she said. Turning abruptly, she crossed the yard to her own house.

She swallowed the sharp feeling that rose in her throat. Charlotte liked William because of the way he was, she thought. And she thought of Hogie and the way he was. It was a disloyal thought and she put it out of her mind. She walked a little faster, and opened the door into the house.

Her mother, with a pile of freshly ironed clothing in her arms, stopped to smile at Lu. "I have your blouses sprinkled, Lu. If you want to iron them — "

"Okay," said Lu without expression, and her mother looked at her a moment before going out of the room.

Lu picked up a dampened roll from the clothes-basket, shook it out, and fitted the shoulder of the garment over the ironing board. She ironed carefully, putting her whole mind on it.

Mrs. Martin came back into the kitchen and turned up the burner under the pot of coffee.

"Ironing is the nicest part of housekeeping," her mother said. "It's easy and peaceful and gives you time to think."

Lu looked up. That's exactly what she didn't want to do. "I don't think ironing is so much fun," she said.

"That's because you are fifteen and I am older," Mrs. Martin said.

Lu looked at her mother's face. She didn't sound unhappy about being old. It came to Lu with somewhat of a shock that her mother wasn't really old at all.

"How old were you when you met Daddy?" she asked.

Her mother took a cup down from the shelf and poured herself some coffee. She sat down, smiling with a memory. "About your age, I guess, or perhaps even a little younger."

Lu ironed the collar of the blouse twice before she said, "How did you know it was Daddy who was the right one for you?"

Her mother set the cup down. "I didn't know at all," she said. "As a matter of fact, I didn't even know I liked him until we were in college. He graduated one year ahead of me. And that last year of college was the unhappiest year of my life."

Lu set down the iron. "Why?"

"Because he wasn't there," her mother said.

That was a whole generation ago, Lu reflected. Things were much different then. She went back to her ironing.

"We think alike," said her mother thoughtfully, as

she sipped her coffee. "That's not to say that we don't have our differences of opinion . . ."

Lu looked up quickly.

" — but in the main, we think alike."

Lu went on ironing.

Her mother gazed at her. "You'll be taking a college aptitude test at high school soon, won't you?"

Lu put the blouse on a hanger. "I guess so," she said and hung the blouse on the doorknob.

The front door slammed.

"Angie?" called Mrs. Martin.

Angie came into the kitchen. "I'm in a hurry, Mom. I've got to go get my pay from Hogie." He said it very importantly.

"You'd better take a glass of milk first," said Mrs. Martin.

Angie drank the milk hurriedly. "Did Hogie say anything about me today?" he asked Lu. He refilled the glass.

"No," said Lu, and suddenly she felt pulled two ways. On one hand, she wanted Angie to get his telescope; on the other, she was angry at Hogie for giving him a way to do it. She tried to smile. What came out was a grimace — half smile, half frown.

Angie said, "I wish I were seventeen."

"For heaven's sakes, why?" asked his mother.

"Hogie said you could do anything you want when you're seventeen."

Mrs. Martin looked amused. "Well, I wouldn't say *anything*," she said.

"You can work without a special permit — in a gas station or on a truck. That's what Hogie said."

Lu looked at Angie with a feeling of relief. Hogie must have talked about getting a job, a real job. Perhaps after school and on Saturdays. Shame at herself for doubting him now filled her. No wonder he hadn't cared about the paper route. She regarded Angie with a new-felt fondness. "You don't have to help me with the dishes tonight," she said impulsively.

"You mean it?" Angie set his milk down in surprise.

"Of course!" she said. She felt her mother's eyes on her, too, and pretended to look out the window at something next door.

"As soon as you collect your money, you come right Home," Mrs. Martin called after Angie as he went out the door.

The telephone rang, and Lu ran to answer it.

"Hey! I missed you!" Hogie said.

Lu smiled into the telephone. "I know," she said but did not bother to explain.

"Look," he said, "meet me at the Coke shop at five, will you? I have something to tell you."

Lu laughed low and happily. She guessed it would be about the job.

"All right," she said. "I'll see you."

Her mother was looking at her.

"I think I'll go over to see Charlotte a moment," she said with studied unconcern, and opened the back door. She ran down the steps and walked blissfully over to Charlotte's house.

17

CHARLOTTE flung open the door at Lu's light knock.

"They took the pig!" she cried. "They came and took the pig. They didn't even wait for William. They just picked it up and stuck it into a sack and took it!"

Lu patted her friend's shoulder. "It had to go back some day," she said. "You knew it would have to."

Charlotte nodded and sniffed. "He was such a nice pig," she said, beginning to cry. "William — " she hiccuped, "William was crazy about him."

Lu removed her arm from around her friend's back, and gazed at her. Charlotte was crying about William, and not about the pig. Lu tried not to smile.

Charlotte turned to Lu, her eyes full of tears. "You don't know," she said. "You really don't know."

"Yes, I do," Lu whispered. "I really do."

"I've been cooking him a big bowl of mush, myself, every morning," said Charlotte.

The doorbell rang. Charlotte wiped her eyes with her arm and went to the door.

"William!" Lu heard Charlotte say.

William cleared his throat a time or two. "I thought I'd stop over and — "

"The pig's gone!" said Charlotte.

"Is that so?" said William. There was an awkward pause. "Well, to tell you the truth, I knew he was gone. I came over to see you."

Lu backed out of the living room, tiptoed through the dining room, and went out the back way. She smiled as she thought of Charlotte and William. And she smiled some more when she thought of Hogie and herself. Hogie and herself, William and Charlotte — any way she said it, it seemed to come out just right.

She glanced up at the overcast skies, and felt the first scattered drops of rain on her head. She smiled broadly then, and shook them out of her hair and face, and bounded into the house before they could deluge her. Lu opened the kitchen door just as the rain began to splatter hard on the porch steps.

Angie was home, but she didn't see him at once. He was standing in the middle of the kitchen with his back to her, a scrawny bird with ears, she thought. She smiled fondly as she closed the door behind her.

"Did you see Hogie?" She smiled some more as she spoke his name.

"I saw him."

There was something odd about his tone, thought Lu. He turned around. Lu looked at him in surprise. His face was smudgy. She wondered suddenly if he had been crying about the pig too.

"What's the matter?"

129

Angie's shoulders rolled, two bony wings under his striped T-shirt. He stuck his hands into his pockets.

"He didn't pay me," he said.

"You mean — Hogie?"

Angie pulled a hand out of his pocket. He showed her what was in it. "He gave me that!" he said. "He kept the rest himself."

Lu gazed at the pennies in his outstretched hand. She thought of Hogie letting Angie fold his papers for him, and carry the bag, and deliver the Sunday route by himself. She thought of the mornings Angie had jumped out of bed, those early dark mornings —

"Hogie did that?" she whispered.

"All he gave me was that!" Angie flung the money from him out into the room, and with a strangled cry, threw his arm over his face and stumbled up the stairs to his room.

Lu's glance followed a penny which rolled on its edge slowly across the floor.

Hogie was a cheat, she thought painfully. He thought it was smart to take advantage of a kid like Angie. All at once she remembered his not getting up to do his job of delivering the newspapers; she remembered his losing his license; she remembered the books he had never bothered to return or pay for. He's lazy, she thought, and careless, and irresponsible. He was not the way she thought he was at all. And she blamed him for that.

The rolling coin disappeared under the stove. Lu got down on her hands and knees and pulled it out. She gathered up the other coins, setting them carefully on the kitchen table. It was almost five. She had told Hogie she would meet him at five. Pressing her lips into a firm straight line, Lu stood looking down at the coins on the table.

Then she went to the hall closet, put on her coat, tied her scarf securely around her head, and went out.

18

Lᴜ ᴡᴀʟᴋᴇᴅ rapidly in the direction of the Coke shop. "I got to know him before I got to like him" — Charlotte's words echoed irrelevantly in her mind. She gave her head a shake, thrust her hands deep into her pockets and went on.

The rain cloud still hovered overhead, and she ducked her head into the wind which was pushing it across the sky. *Hogie making fun of the teacher the first day he came to school* — remembering, Lu wondered why she hadn't seen it then the very first day. Or if not just then — later when he had so carefully knocked over the books to bother the librarian. She remembered how she had just as good as closed her eyes to his pushing in out of turn. Lu grimaced at the sky. She guessed that's what she had been doing all along — closing her eyes. She hadn't seen any of it the way it really was.

The clouds that had been rolling across the sky left a patch of clear blue. The sun momentarily beamed down upon Lu, flashing a warm smile, before it was again covered up by a cloud. Lu pulled off her scarf and stuffed it into her pocket. She crossed the street.

He was waiting for her out of the rain inside the Coke shop. Coolly she looked at him through the big window. He saw her at once and smiled the lopsided smile that had seemed to promise so much so long ago. He rushed out to greet her.

"Hi," he said, taking her arm. He hurried her to the street crossing. "I want to tell you something," he said.

"I want to tell you something, too," she said, but he was too eager to make it across the street to notice her dry tone.

At the vacant bench, at the bus stop, they sat down.

"I'm quitting school," said Hogie.

Lu turned suddenly in surprise. "You can't!" she gasped.

"Sure I can," said Hogie. "The law says you have to stay in school until you're sixteen." He patted the wallet she had given him which stuck out of his jacket pocket. "I'm more than sixteen," he said.

"Your father — " she said.

"He doesn't care. Anyway, I've got a job." He said it proudly. "In a furniture factory. I start tomorrow."

"You mean you won't finish high school?" Her voice was incredulous.

"I've got a job," he repeated. "What's the use of finishing high school?"

"But you're just a sophomore," she said. "Just like me! I'm not even grown up yet!"

His eyes flicked over her. "You look plenty grown up to me," he said.

133

She flushed. They weren't talking about the same thing. Suddenly she knew they had never talked about the same thing, not even when they had talked about the weather.

She said firmly, "Don't be silly, Hogie. You can't quit before you've even finished high school."

He laughed at her, as if what she said was funny to him. He took out a coin from his pocket and tossed it into the air.

Her eyes followed the coin's flight. Then she remembered. "You forgot to pay my brother for the paper route," she said.

He tucked the coin back into his pocket. "I didn't forget," he said.

She licked her lips. "You didn't pay him — enough."

He looked at her, surprised.

"When you made him substitute, he figured you'd pay him the full amount for the papers he delivered."

"That isn't what I figured," Hogie said. "I didn't ask him to come along — he asked me!"

She said hotly, "But that isn't fair!"

"Look honey," he said, "that's plain business. Sure he's your brother and all that — but his mamma can't protect him all his life. He has to learn to take care of himself."

She only looked at him.

He met her gaze fully. "I didn't cheat him," he said, and she saw that he believed it. "I never told him I'd pay him anything at all. I gave him something because I like him — he's a good kid."

She smiled wryly. "Thanks a lot," she said.

The rain began to drop again, so finely that it was like a perfume spray against her skin. She tipped back her head feeling it in a mist on her cheeks.

"Looks like rain again," said Hogie, glancing up at the sky with a grimace. He took his green hat from his back pocket, and fitted it carefully down over his head.

"It's all in the way you look at it, I guess," said Lu, and she might have been speaking only of the weather. She stood up.

Hogie jumped up to stand beside her. "I'll have my car back Monday," he said. "I'll pick you up at noon and we'll ride around for a while."

She shook her head. "It's against the rules to leave the school grounds at noon," she said.

He twisted his smile at her. "The rules never bothered you much before."

She examined the truth of that. She had made excuses for him — and fooled only herself. She returned his gaze candidly.

"I thought you were always breaking the rules because you didn't know about them. I didn't think it was because you didn't really care."

He stared at her a moment.

"I get it," he said. "You don't want to ride with me — ever."

She said, her voice clear — "We don't think alike.

It's just that we don't think alike."

He really didn't know what she was talking about, she saw from the expression on his face.

"I'm sorry." She turned away.

His voice came after her, puzzled. "Hey!" he said. "You want your wallet back?"

She shook her head, and walked rapidly away.

She ran the last block home. For she had decided what she would do. She would return the quarts of unopened paint and give Angie the money due him. She rushed up the stairs and down the hall, and flung open the door of her room. She looked around with surprise.

The gold walls had turned to mustard color in the gray light. The white bedspread gapped in the center with its basted seam. The bathroom rug on the floor by her bed was simply a bathroom rug. Lu's eyes settled on the lamps. Only by closing her eyes could she see them as anything but shades wrapped in brown paper which had been hastily, and not too neatly, swabbed with gold paint. Lu shook herself a little.

She had never really *looked* at it before, she decided, and was struck suddenly with the similarity to the other truth. She had never really looked at Hogie as he was, either.

She couldn't blame him, she saw now. She couldn't blame Hogie for being the way he was; she could only blame herself for not seeing him truly. Every time she had looked at him, counting back to

136

the day he had walked into the room, she had only seen what she wanted to see. She had never really seen *him*. Lu tried to recall the picture she had had in her mind before she met Hogie. But it was no longer there. It had been only a dream. Lu stared at herself thoughtfully in the mirror.

"Lu?" Her mother stopped at the doorway and looked into the room. Lu turned. She saw her mother shudder delicately, and deliberately focus her attention on Lu's face.

Lu grinned. "It's pretty terrible, isn't it?"

Mrs. Martin looked at her closely, curiously for a moment, before the corners of her mouth quivered into a smile.

"It's been a strain to keep my hands off," she admitted. "Your father was sure you'd see it yourself one day."

Lu thought of her father and her throat began to hurt. He hadn't hollered at her when she had fallen down in her grades. He had merely talked quietly and put it up to her fairly. He had expected her to follow through on her own responsibility. She swallowed. Suddenly it no longer seemed so unnecessary to pay attention to Miss Egbert.

She said then, as if they had been talking of it all along — "Well, I won't be going out with him anymore."

Her mother merely nodded. "I went ahead and

finished your ironing," she said, handing her the blouse she had been carrying on its hanger.

Lu stared at the garment a moment. "Thank you, Mother," she said slowly. "Thank you very much." But it wasn't the ironing she was thinking of. It wasn't that at all.

And it was with no feeling of surprise that she perceived that her mother somehow knew exactly what she meant.